Also by Mary Costello

The China Factory

Academy Street

Academy Street

Mary Costello

Farrar, Straus and Giroux
New York

Farrar, Straus and Giroux
18 West 18th Street, New York 10011

Printed in the United States of America
Originally published in 2014 by Canongate, Great Britain
Published in the United States by Farrar, Straus and Giroux
First American edition, 2015

Library of Congress Cataloging-in-Publication Data
Costello, Mary, [date]
    Academy street : a novel / Mary Costello. — First American
edition.
        pages   cm
    ISBN 978-0-374-10052-0 (hardcover) —
    ISBN 978-0-374-71275-4 (ebook)
    1. Irish women—Fiction.   2. Irish Americans—New York
(State)—New York—Fiction.   3. Families—Ireland—Fiction.
I. Title.

PR6103.O85 A65 2015
823'.92—dc23

2014023448

Designed by Abby Kagan

Farrar, Straus and Giroux books may be purchased for educational, business, or
promotional use. For information on bulk purchases, please contact the
Macmillan Corporate and Premium Sales Department at 1-800-221-7945,
extension 5442, or write to specialmarkets@macmillan.com.

www.fsgbooks.com
www.twitter.com/fsgbooks • www.facebook.com/fsgbooks

1   3   5   7   9   10   8   6   4   2

For my mother,
Ann

and her sisters,
Carmel and Clare

In the depths of the winter
I finally learned that there lay in me
an unconquerable summer.

—Albert Camus

Part One

1 It is evening and the window is open a little. There are voices in the hall, footsteps running up and down the stairs, then along the back corridor towards the kitchen. Now and then Tess hears the crunch of gravel outside, the sound of a bell as a bicycle is laid against the wall. Earlier a car drove up the avenue, into the yard, and horses and traps too, the horses whinnying as they were pulled up. She is sitting on the dining-room floor in her good dress and shoes. The sun is streaming in through the tall windows, the light falling on the floor, the sofa, the marble hearth. She holds her face up to feel its warmth.

For two days people have been coming and going and now there is something near. She wishes everyone would go home and let the house be quiet again. The summer is gone. Every day the leaves fall off the trees and blow down the avenue. She thinks of them blowing into the courtyard, past the coach house, under the stone arch. In the morning she had gone out to the orchard and stood inside the high wall. It was cold then. The pear tree stood alone. She walked under the apple trees. She picked up a rotten yellow apple, and when she smelled it, it reminded her of the apple room and the apples laid out on newspapers on the floor, turning yellow.

She lies back on the rug and looks up at the pictures on the wallpaper. Adam and Eve in the Garden of Eden. Her mother told her the story. She picks out the colors—dark green, blue, red—and follows the ivy trailing all over the wallpaper, all around Adam and Eve. They are both naked except for a few leaves. Eve has a frightened look on her face. She has just spotted the serpent. A serpent is a snake, her mother said. The apple tree behind Eve is old and bent, like the ones in the orchard.

She feels something in the room. A whishing sound, and a little breeze rushes past her. She sits up, blinks. A blackbird has flown into the room. It flies around and around and she smiles, amazed, and opens her arms for it to come to her. It perches on the top of the china cabinet and watches her with one eye. Then it takes off again and comes to rest on the wooden pelmet above the curtains. It starts to peck at a spot on the wall. She holds her breath. She listens to the tap-tap of its beak, then a faint tearing sound and a little strip of wallpaper comes away and the bird with the little strip like a twig in its beak rises and circles and flies out the window. She looks after it, astonished.

The door opens and the head of her sister Claire appears. "Is this where you are? *Tess!* Come on, hurry on!"

Something is about to happen. Her older sisters, Evelyn and Claire, are home from boarding school. She loves Claire almost as much as her mother, or Captain the dog. More than she loves Evelyn, or Maeve, her other sister, or even the baby. Equal to how she loves Mike Connolly, the workman.

The door opens again, and Claire holds out her hand urgently for Tess to come. There are people standing around the hall, waiting. The front door is wide open and outside there are more people. She can hear their feet crunching the gravel and the hum of low talk. She looks around at the faces of her aunts and cousins, her neighbors. Her teacher, Mrs. Snee, is smiling at her. Claire pulls her close—they are standing next to Aunt Maud now—and squeezes her hand and bows her head. Suddenly she is frightened.

A shuffle on the upstairs landing and everyone goes quiet. Men's voices, half whispering but urgent, drift down from above. She thinks there must be a lot of people up there but when she looks up there are only shadows and shoulders beyond the banisters. She sighs. She will soon need to go to the bathroom. She looks down at her new shoes. She got them in Briggs's shop in the town during the school holidays, along with the green dress she is wearing. Her mother got new shoes that day too. And a new blue dress. Her mother bent down to tie her laces and Tess left her hand on her mother's head, on the soft hair.

The stairs sweep up and turn to the right and it is here on the turn, by the stained-glass window, that her uncle's back comes into view. Light is streaming in. Her heart starts to beat fast. She sees the back of a neighbor, Tommy Burns, and her other uncle, struggling. And then she understands. At the exact moment she sees the coffin, she understands. It turns the corner and the sun hits it. The sun flows all over the coffin, turning the wood yellow and red and orange like the window, lighting it up, making it beautiful. The gold handles are shining. It is so beautiful, her heart swells and floods with the light. She closes her eyes. She can feel her mother near. Her mother is reaching out a hand, smiling at her. She can feel the touch of her mother's fingers on her face. Her mother is all hers—her face, her long hair, her mouth, they are all hers. Then someone coughs and she opens her eyes.

The men are almost at the bottom of the stairs and the coffin is tilted, heavy. She is afraid it will fall. Her father and her older brother, Denis, get behind it now, lifting, helping. She looks down, presses her toes against the soles of her shoes to keep her feet still. She wants to run up the last few steps and open the coffin and bring her mother out. She looks at the handles again, and at the little crosses on the top. She tries to count them. There is a big gold cross on the lid. Last night, when her cousin Kathleen took her up to bed, they passed her mother's room. The shutters were closed and candles were lit. There were people standing and sitting and leaning against the walls, neighbors, relations, all saying the Rosary. She dipped her head to see past the crowd. She could not see her mother. Just the dark wood of the wardrobe and the washstand. And the mirror covered with a black cloth. And leaning up against the wall, against the pink roses of the wallpaper, the wooden lid with the gold cross, and the light of the candles dancing on it. They put the lid on over her mother. She looks up at Claire, about to speak, but Claire says "Shh," and tightens her grip on Tess's hand. A silence falls on the hall. She turns and sees the big brass gong that she and Maeve play with sometimes by the wall. She wants to reach for the beater and hit the gong hard.

The coffin is crawling towards the front door. Then the men leave it down on two chairs and rest for a minute. When they pick it up again, everyone walks behind it and it passes through the open door, into the sun. On the gravel there is a black hearse and a thousand faces looking at them. The men bring the coffin to the back of the hearse and shove it in through the open door, like into a mouth. Maeve starts to cry and Claire goes to her.

Tess turns and sees Mike Connolly at the edge of the yard, with Captain the dog at his feet. He is holding his cap in his hand. She thinks he is crying. Everyone is crying, but she is not. She looks up and sees the blackbird on the laurel tree, eyeing her. *You robber*, she wants to shout, *you tore my mother's wallpaper, and now she's dead*. She looks past the white railings that run around the lawn, over the sloping fields and the quarry, far off to a clump of trees. Then the hearse door is shut and she gets a jolt. She looks around. She does not know what to do. The evening sun is blinding her. It is shining on everything, too bright, on the laurel tree and the lawn and the white railings, on the hearse and the gravel and the blackbird.

The hearse pulls away and people start walking behind it.

Her uncle's car follows and then the horses and traps, and the neighbors, wheeling bicycles. Claire is beside her again, leaning into her face. "You've to go into the house, Tess. You and Maeve, ye're to stay at home with Kathleen."

Her cousin Kathleen takes her hand, leads herself and Maeve around to the side of the house, down the steps into the small yard. Before they reach the back door, Tess breaks away and runs back across the gravel, the lawn, off into the fields. On a small hill she stands and watches the hearse moving up the avenue, turning onto the main road. It moves along the stone wall that circles her father's land, the crowd and the horses and traps walking after it. Sometimes the trees or the wall block her view. But she watches, and waits, until the black roof of the hearse comes into view again, flashing in the sun. It slows and turns left onto Chapel Road, and the people follow, like dark shapes. Then they begin to disappear.

She stands still, watching until the last shape fades and she is alone. She is gone. Her mother is gone. She feels a little sick, dizzy from the huge sky above. She feels the ground falling away from under her—the grass and the field and the hill are all sliding away, until she is left high and dry on the top of a bare hill. Like the Blessed Virgin in the picture in the church when she is taken up into Heaven from the top of a mountain. Maybe she, Tess, is being taken up into Heaven this very minute. She can hardly breathe. She turns her face towards the low sun and closes her eyes and waits. *Please.* She waits for her mother's face to appear, a hand to reach out. She leans her whole body upwards, desperate for the sun to touch her, the wind to raise her, the sky to open, Heaven to pull her in.

When she opens her eyes she is still in her father's field, and there, a few feet away, are cattle, five or six, staring at her with big faces and sad eyes. The ground is under her feet again, the grass is green, nothing has changed. She looks around, frightened, ashamed. She starts running back towards the house. She runs into the yard, searches the barn, the coach house, the stables. She sticks her head into the dark musty potato house and calls out, "Mike, Mike, are you there?" and waits and listens. Everywhere is silent. Soon it will be dark. She hears the sound of a motor in the distance. A car is coming down the avenue. She stands and waits for it to appear in the yard. Her heart is pounding. It is the hearse, she thinks, returning. With her mother sitting up in the front seat, smiling, and the coffin behind open, empty—a terrible mistake put right. They had come to the wrong house. They had come for the wrong woman—it was old Mrs. Geraghty back in the village they should have taken.

But it is not the hearse that drives into the yard. It is Miss Tannian, the poultry instructress. She steps out of her car in a green tweed costume and patent shoes. And auburn hair, like Tess's mother's. The sky is pink and as she comes towards Tess the last of the sun lights her up from behind. She is speaking to Tess, saying, *I am sorry, I am so sorry.* Tess runs away from her, off along the edge of the yard, under the arch towards the orchard. The big iron gates are open and she runs in and stands in the shadows. The apple trees are dark, their low crooked branches like old women's skirts. Her eyes dart all over the place, along the four high walls. And then she sees him, Mike Connolly, sitting on an old stump at the far end, his head down, Captain beside him. As soon as she sees him the tears come. She runs and falls at his feet and begins to sob.

It is dark when the others come home. Her aunt Maud and Maud's husband, Frank, and the aunts and cousins from Dublin crowd into the kitchen. The Tilley lamps are lit. There are all kinds of nice things on the pantry shelves, cakes and buns and biscuits. Mrs. Glynn, who took the baby over to her house, is here. She helps Tess's sisters serve tea and sandwiches to all the guests, and whiskey to the men. Her father sits quietly in the armchair. Her brother Denis has his head down. Tess wants to climb up on his lap like she used to when she was four. They are talking about the baby, Oliver. Aunt Maud says she will take him.

"It'll be for the best," she says.

Her father says nothing.

"It'll only be for a year or two," Aunt Maud says. "And sure ye'll be over and back, and Kathleen can bring him back every Sunday to play with the girls." She looks around the table. "That's settled, so. And isn't it what she wanted herself?"

"It is," her father says at last. "It's what she wanted, all right."

She goes up to the front hall and drags a stool over to open the door. It is dark outside. She sits on the step and folds her arms. She can make out the laurel tree on the lawn. She remembers when she and Maeve came home from school every day, her mother sitting under the shiny laurel tree with a blanket around her knees, sewing, and Oliver beside her in his cradle. Sometimes her head was down, sleeping. Oliver wasn't long born and he was sleeping too. Tess would run to them and look in over the top of his cradle and smell his baby smell. Her mother's long hair was tied back. Then she would get a fit of coughing and her hair would come loose. Once there was blood in her hankie. When she was in bed, sick, her hair was let down. They took Tess up to her mother's room last week and her mother was sitting up in her white nightdress. They lifted her onto the high bed and her mother kissed her forehead. But then, when Tess started to stroke her mother's hair and lie against her, Evelyn said, Come on, down with you now, madam, and she took her away.

Tess has not had her tea. She wonders who will make their teas now. She likes a boiled egg and currant bread with butter.

She likes when her mother stands beside her father at the table and pours him a cup of steaming tea from the teapot. Sometimes, he puts out his hand and touches her mother's bottom and she and her sisters pretend not to see. Her mother is in her coffin in the chapel tonight. God will probably drop down His Golden Chute soon—any minute now—when He is ready to take her mother up into Heaven. That is how she, Tess, and her brothers and sisters arrived on earth. Her mother told her that whenever she and Tess's father wanted a new baby, she went to the chapel and there she prayed, and God, hearing her prayer, dropped down His Golden Chute and popped in a baby and down the chute the baby flew, fat and happy and gurgling, into her mother's waiting arms.

Tess takes off her shoes, looks up at the black sky, begins to hum. She is not sure if the Golden Chute actually takes people back up into Heaven. That is a guess. She wonders if her mother is on her way, now, this minute, moving through the dark sky, in and out among the cold stars. She grows a little afraid. She looks down at her hands. She picks at the old burn mark on her thumb. She bites off a bit of skin and chews it. She remembers the day she got the burn. Oliver wasn't even born and she had not started school. She went out with her mother to feed the hens. Chuck, chuck, chuck, they called out. They went into the duckhouse and the henhouse to gather the eggs. Her mother had a bucket and Tess had a small tin can. Tess wanted to be just like her mother. When her mother put the eggs in her bucket that day, Tess wanted eggs in her tin can too. She started to cry, but then her mother said, Look, look, and she picked up three lovely shiny stones from the yard and put them into Tess's can and rattled them around. Then her mother ran off inside, in case the bread got burnt. Tess ran after her, but she saw another lovely pebble shining up at her from the ground and she stopped and put it in her tin can and raced in through the small yard, calling out to her mother about her new pebble. At the back door she tripped and tumbled down the steps into the kitchen, and then, half running, she fell sideways into the open fire. Her mother cried out and let the griddle pan fall and ran and lifted Tess and swung her across the kitchen into the big white sink. Later, telling Tess's father what had happened, her mother began to cry. Her two little hands were burnt, she told him, wiping her eyes. Tess tried to show him the pebbles but her hands were all bandaged up.

Everyone dresses in black the next morning and goes to the funeral. Tess and Maeve stay behind with Mike Connolly. The dining-room table is set with the good china and cutlery. There's a leg of mutton cooked and left aside in the kitchen. Mrs. Glynn comes with warm brown bread. She takes off her coat and puts eggs on to boil. She tells Maeve to mash up cold potatoes with a fork. When the plates are ready, Tess and Maeve carry them up to the dining room. Mrs. Glynn puts on her coat and says if she hurries she'll make the burial. Tess's heart jumps. Mrs. Glynn takes Maeve with her, but Tess is too young to go to the graveyard. "Your poor mother," she says. Before they leave Tess asks about Oliver. When is Oliver coming home? Mrs. Glynn says they can come and see him tomorrow. He'll be going to live with Aunt Maud after that.

When they are gone the house is quiet. The smell of the mutton makes her feel sick. She listens to the clock ticking. Everything is changing. No one puts the wireless on anymore. She hears water dripping inside the pipes high up on the wall. Upstairs the floorboards are creaking. She starts to grow afraid. She is sure there is someone up there. She thinks her mother will come down the stairs and into the kitchen. She runs out into the small yard and as she turns the corner onto the lawn she crashes into Mike Connolly. "Ah, *a leanbh*, slow down, slow down."

"I think Momma is coming down the stairs, Mike, I think she's back. I heard her steps."

"Come on in now out of that, and make me some tea. My belly's above in my back. D'you know how many cows I milked this morning, do you? Before you even turned over for your second sleep, Missy!"

He throws two sods of turf on the fire, and hangs the kettle on the crane. The clock is quieter now. Outside, the crows are cawing. Mike is standing, looking into the fire, and she does the same. When the flames are big and red and the kettle is singing, he makes a pot of tea. He cuts the bread and says, "Will we make a bit of toast?" She smiles. He knows—like her mother knows—that toast is her favorite, favorite thing in the world. He sticks a cut of bread on a fork and leans in and holds it before the flames. She leans in too. Their faces grow pink and warm as the bread turns brown. He toasts three or four cuts and neither of them says a word. But she is happy. She is happy. They sit together at the big table and he butters her toast and spreads jam on it and her mouth waters. He pours two cups of tea and gives her a wink. "Eat up now," he says. And then, just as he is about to take a bite, he turns his head and sees something and a change comes over him. She follows his look to her mother's apron hanging on a nail at the end of the dresser. It is floury around the belly from all the times her mother leaned against the table, kneading the bread. "Eat up, Mike," she says quickly. "Your toast is getting cold."

They have all come back, the priest too, and they are sitting at the long table up in the dining room. Tess keeps an eye on the small china milk jugs, and when they are empty she runs all the way back to the kitchen and refills them. She moves along the table offering buns and shop cake from a plate. Her hair is tied back neatly. She stands straight, smiling politely when she is praised. The priest asks her how old she is. Seven, she tells him. He says she's a great girl and that she's the image of her mother and in that second her heart nearly bursts with happiness. She looks across the room, up at the spot above the window where the bird tore the wallpaper. She wants to run and find her mother and tell her what the priest just said.

Her father sits at one end of the table, the priest at the other.

"May the Lord have mercy on her soul," the priest says. "What age was she, Michael?"

Her father stops eating. "Nineteen hundred and four, she was born. She was forty last March. That's when she started to complain. Just after the child was born."

He looks around them all, then at the priest. "I met a nun once in a church in Galway," he says. "She was back from America. D'you know what she told me? She said that a man's soul weighs the same as a snipe. Some scientist over there weighed people just before they died, TB patients she said, and then he weighed them again just after they died, beds and all. And weren't they lighter? . . . Imagine that . . . The soul was gone, she said."

Aunt Maud blows her nose into her handkerchief. Evelyn goes around the table with the teapot, then whispers something to Aunt Maud.

"She told Evelyn where to get the linen tablecloth to put on the table for the meal," Aunt Maud says. "Isn't that right, Evelyn?"

Evelyn nods and sniffs. "She did. Only a few days ago. She told me which drawer it was in."

Tess is watching her father. He takes a drink of tea and swallows. All the time he is looking down. She can see the bones in his face moving under his skin.

"She was a fine woman," the priest says. "A fine woman."

"She even told us which dress to lay her out in—her new blue dress," Evelyn says.

Tess's heart nearly stops. She understands what that means; her mother is lying in her coffin in her new blue dress. The one she got in Briggs's that day that Tess got her dress, the one she is wearing now. Carefully, she leaves the cake plate up on the sideboard and walks out of the dining room on shaky legs. She climbs the stairs. The sun is flooding in through the stained-glass window, like yesterday. She hurries past, to the upstairs landing and down along the corridor to her parents' room. The door is closed. She stands for a moment, then turns the handle and walks in. It is dark. The drapes have not been opened. There is a bad smell, like when a mouse dies under the floorboards. She runs and drags open the drapes on one of the windows. The mirror is still covered with the black cloth. On the dressing table there is a photograph of her father and mother on their wedding day. She looks at it. Her father might get a new wife now. She might get a new mother. There is another photograph of her mother in a nurse's uniform when she was young and working in a hospital down in Cork. She opens the top drawer, lifts out a red cloth box, checks her mother's brooches, her locket, her hat pins. Nothing is missing. She opens the wardrobe door and gets a terrible fright. For a second she thinks there are people in funeral clothes standing inside the wardrobe. She pushes at the coats and the dresses but there are too many and she is too small and they fall back in her way again. She pulls and drags on the hems of the dresses and skirts, bringing them towards the light. She is almost crying. There is no blue dress. Her mother is wearing it in the coffin. Then she remembers that her mother is no longer in the chapel. She is down in the ground now. Or up in Heaven.

In the dark she is counting sheep, like Claire told her to do. It is no good, she cannot sleep. She starts to count all the days since she was born, but it is too hard. She tries to remember every single day, every single minute with her mother. Suddenly, there is a loud bang. She sits up, terrified. She hears dogs barking in the distance. Maeve does not stir in her bed across the room. Then everything is silent again. She listens out for sounds in the house. A big bright moon is shining into the room, making everything white, even the floorboards. *Mellow the moonlight.* When the woman comes on the wireless singing this song, her mother sings along. *There's a form at the casement, a form of her true love. And he whispered with face bent, I'm waiting for you love.* Tess meant to ask her mother what a casement was, and a form. Her mother said there is a man in the moon and Tess kneels up on her bed now and looks out the window, turning her head this way and that, trying to make out his face.

In the morning before it is fully bright she wakes up. She listens out for Oliver. And then she remembers and a sick feeling comes over her. Early each morning last summer the little birds used to sing, huddled together under the roof above her window. Now they are all gone; their wings and tiny hearts are grown up. She closes her eyes, tries to go back to sleep. The house is so quiet she thinks everyone might be gone and she is the only one left. She pulls the blankets up to her chin to keep out the cold.

She sits up, looks across at Maeve sleeping. She gets out of bed and runs over to the big window, hardly feeling the floor under her. The sky is gray and low, everything still asleep. She looks out across the lawn, then far off over the fields. Her father is coming over a hill, in his long coat, with a gun on his shoulder. He is carrying dead rabbits. He comes nearer and nearer. She has never seen him like this, so lonely.

2 They are running down the road to Glynn's. Running, she feels free. In her bare legs, in the rush of air, she feels strong and free. She keeps up with Maeve, happy, almost dancing, almost forgetting what has happened. The door opens and Mrs. Glynn walks out with Oliver in her arms. They run to him, cooing, and take him into their own arms. Inside, they sit on a rug and eat bread and jam and play with Oliver until they all grow tired and quiet.

Just when her thoughts start to come against her and she remembers why she is here, there is a knock on the door. A family of tinkers stands outside. Maeve and Tess gather close to Mrs. Glynn. "God bless this house and all in it," the tinker woman says in a rough voice. She has a baby in her arms and three or four children beside her. A girl of about Tess's age is chewing the ends of her hair. She stops chewing and looks at Tess in a way that makes Tess look away. Out on the road the tinker man and three older boys wait with the donkey and cart. Tess recognizes the tinker man. He came to the school one day and cleaned out the lavatories. The tinker woman holds out an empty tin can now, begging for milk or anything they can spare. Her big brown face and her rough voice and all the wild children frighten Tess and she cannot wait for them to go away again.

She stands at the window and watches them crowd onto the cart and squat down. As they pull away it starts to rain. The girl is behind, facing back, and she catches Tess's eye again and stares at her. Tess feels cold and strange. She is afraid the girl will put a spell on her. She thinks the tinker girl knows something about her, something that Tess herself does not know. The girl straightens up. Her eyes lock onto Tess's. Slowly, she sticks out her tongue. Tess's heart almost stops. It is meant for her and her alone. She is doomed, cursed. The cart rounds a bend and disappears out of sight.

The next evening Aunt Maud comes and brings Oliver away. They have packed up all his things. Tess watches as their uncle Frank's car drives away. She walks around the house, trying to find a place that will make her feel right again. She goes to all her favorite rooms, to the space under the back stairs, the orchard. But happiness does not return. Nothing will do away with this feeling she is carrying inside her, like a bad secret.

Her older sisters, Evelyn and Claire, do not return to boarding school. On their first morning back at national school Claire walks Tess and Maeve to the end of the avenue. They have mutton sandwiches and shop cake, left over from the funeral, for their lunches. They walk along the road to the end of their father's farm. Tess grows nervous; she is not sure they will be safe venturing this far from home. She looks into a field where the cattle are butting heads and jumping on each other's backs.

In the school yard the children form a circle around herself and Maeve, and for a little while she feels special. Is your mammy dead? they ask. She wonders if there is a way people can tell now. "Did ye touch her—was she as cold as marble? Where's she buried?" one of the big boys asks. Kildoon, Maeve says. "That's where Seán Blake's granny is buried. Her grave was robbed," he says.

"They dug up her coffin and took the rings off her fingers and the pennies off her eyes." He looks straight at Tess. Then the bell rings.

She is allowed to sit with Maeve in the senior classroom today. Before the lesson begins, Mr. Clarke the headmaster picks up an egg from his desk and turns his back on the children and cracks it open. He throws back his head and swallows the raw egg in one gulp. A rainbow appears in the sky and he writes the seven colors on the blackboard and raps his cane as the children chant out the words. She sits close to Maeve, their arms touching. She is stiff with fear. She cannot read so she tries hard to remember the colors. *Red, orange, yellow, green, blue, indigo, and violet*, she calls, flinching at each rap of the cane.

On the way home they pass the tinkers' camp at the Black Bend. The dogs start to bark. The trees are leaning low and dark, but she can see the tents and the fires and children crying and running around in their bare feet. A man is sitting on an upside-down bucket, hammering a tin can. There are rags drying on bushes, and a horse and a donkey tied to a tree. "Hurry on," Maeve says in a low voice and they walk quickly. Then Tess sees the girl from the day before, standing outside a tent. She looks smaller, paler. The girl sees Tess too. Tess has the feeling that they know each other, or that they are somehow close, the way sisters are close, and that the girl understands this too. She wants to smile, to show that they are friends. Then she does something—she sticks her tongue out at the tinker girl, just like the girl did yesterday. The girl frowns and looks sad and Tess feels bad. Her heart feels sick. *It was only a game*, she wants to say. But the girl is turning away. She lifts the flap of the tent and enters.

On the avenue they kick at the fallen leaves. A black car drives out of the yard towards them. It is Miss Tannian. She rolls down the window, smiles, asks about their day. She is wearing red lipstick. Tess can feel the eyes of her father and Mike Connolly

from over the wall in the potato field, watching. Denis is bending over the pit in the corner of the field. He is as tall as her father now, but thinner.

"That one is after Dadda," Evelyn says before the men come in to
their dinner. "And Mother not cold in her grave." They are talking about Miss Tannian.

"Don't be daft," Claire says. "She only came to take the blood
and check for reactors."

"Reactors, my eye! Did you see the get-up of her—in the costume and lipstick? And she's no spring chicken either, let me
tell you."

Once, last summer, they had to lock up the hens in the henhouse for testing. It was a big job. Her mother held up each hen
and Miss Tannian drew out blood in a little syringe and squirted
it into small bottles to take away. Then her mother opened the
hatch at the bottom of the henhouse door and flung the hen
out into the yard. Rhode Island Reds and Leghorns. Leghorns
are the best for laying, her mother said.

"Anyway, doesn't she know well Dadda is only after burying
his wife?" Claire said.

"Mark my words—that one is setting her cap at him. She's
after this place. Herself and her cocked nose."

After the dinner Tess goes out to the back hall, past the tap
room and the apple room. She is searching again. She wants to
leave down this secret weight, everything she is carrying in her
heart. She thinks of the tinker girl inside her tent, and she
knows, somehow, that the girl is thinking of her too at this moment. She goes to the dark space under the back stairs, where
the incubator stands empty now. In spring the eggs hatched out
there under a Tilley lamp. She loved the warmth and the glow
of the red lamp. There, she was happy. Every day Evelyn or Claire

or her mother turned the eggs over carefully. Then, one morning, a miracle—two yellow chicks had broken through during the night and were staggering around on thin shaky legs. One day, she stood looking in at the eggs. She had a sudden longing to climb in, fold herself up, lie down under the lovely warm light. Then her mother appeared and leaned in and picked up an egg. She held it up to the window light. "Tess," she whispered. "Come, look at the little birdie inside!" Tess moved close against her mother's body. For a moment she pressed her face against her mother's stomach and closed her eyes and kissed it, and breathed in her smell and she could taste her mother in the smell. When she drew away, her mother was holding the egg up to the light and Tess saw a shadow, the shape of a tiny sleeping bird, inside the shell. She could not speak. Her mother smiled and stroked her head and her heart filled up. Together they stood in a stream of light watching the shadow and then her mother placed the egg back on the straw. She picked up another egg and held it up to the light and frowned, and sighed.

"What's wrong, Momma?" Tess asked.

"No birdie here, sweetheart, no birdie here," she said sadly. "This one's a glugger." She threw it in a bucket for the pigs' feed, and when it burst a terrible rotten smell filled the air.

Two strange men come to the house and fumigate her mother and father's room. They are all tested, even Mike Connolly. That night in bed she remembers Miss Tannian—they have forgotten to test Miss Tannian. She might be their new mother. She does not want a new mother. She misses Oliver. He has come only once since Aunt Maud took him away. Claire made a lovely currant cake for the visit. He had a frown, a new little wrinkle on his forehead. He had looked at Maeve's face, then at Tess's, and back at Maeve's again. They kept smiling and flapping at him but he wasn't sure who they were anymore. Suddenly Tess misses her mother like never before. It is a like a huge wave flowing over her. She misses her mother for herself, and for Oliver too. He does not remember, or understand, why everything is different now. It hurts her heart to think of his small head waking up in Aunt Maud's house, in a room full of cousins and different walls, different voices. A different mother. She thinks of him waking, looking up at the ceiling, or out at the rain. His little heart jumping when a door bangs or a strange face appears, looking in at him through the bars of his crib. That evening of the visit she could not eat the currant cake. It would not go down her throat.

In school she grows to love Mrs. Snee, her teacher, and she knows Mrs. Snee loves her too. Every day she gives her jobs to do. On cold days Mrs. Snee lets the children leave their bottles of milk beside the fire to warm them. Tess doesn't mind leaving home each morning. The house is too quiet now. It is worse when her father comes inside. The wireless has not been turned on since the funeral. Denis cycled to the town one day and got the batteries recharged, but that night when he went to turn it on her father said, "What do you think you're doing?" in a cold hard voice and Denis backed away without a word. She had always been afraid of her father but now it is worse. His face is dark and cross all the time. One night when the priest came to visit she heard her father say, "What's gone is gone." At night he stares into the fire. He does not seem to like anyone—not Denis or Claire or her—except maybe Evelyn. She is the eldest. He gives her housekeeping money every Saturday. She keeps the ration book and sells eggs to the egg man from Henaghan's, and swaps some of the butter she churns for sugar and jam and other groceries that John Joe Donnellan sells in his traveling shop. She sends Denis to the post office, or to town to order chicken feed.

21

Denis is seventeen. He has blue eyes and thick black hair. When he was a baby he was blond like Oliver. They were all blond at the start, her mother said. Denis sits in the kitchen at night, his arms folded, his long legs thrown out in front of him, not saying anything. No one says much anymore. A silence came on the house the day of the funeral and it has stayed. Tess thinks that they would all like the silence to end now, but no one knows how to put an end to it. She looks at their faces at night. She hears her own heart beating in her chest, in her head and ears too, *thump, thump, thump*, deafening her. She watches Denis's chest rising and falling. He can hear his own heart too, she thinks. They can all hear their hearts—Claire and Evelyn and her father—making an awful racket, thumping inside them, like hers.

In the cold, Maeve's feet break out with chilblains and she cries at night. Claire rubs on Zam-Buk and she is kept home from school for two days. Tess goes alone and stays back after school to help Mrs. Snee tidy up. The light is fading when she leaves and her boots begin to hurt. She hurries along the road, almost running, pulling her coat tight. Up ahead is the Black Bend and the tinkers' camp under the trees. She sees the flames of a fire rising and people gathered around—more people than she has ever seen there before, all moving, slow and wavy, in front of the fire. There are men standing at the edge of the camp, smoking and drinking from brown bottles. As she draws nearer, a strange quietness fills the air. Not even the dogs are barking. She stops and looks back the way she has come. The road is empty and she grows afraid. Her eyes meet the eyes of the tinker man who cleaned the school lavatories. He bows his head very slowly and Tess looks away. She walks on, faster, her head down. As she passes in front of the camp, a woman lets out a terrible cry. Tess stands, frozen. There are women and teenage girls gathered in a circle in front of a tent. They look up and see Tess and a hush falls on them. The circle opens and Tess sees a wooden table and on it a child is lying, dressed in white. It is the tinker girl, her eyes closed, her face snow-white, her hands crossed on her chest. She is dead. At the end of the table, a woman is combing the child's hair. It is the tinker woman who came to Mrs. Glynn's door. When she sees Tess, she stops and bows her head. The flames of the fire are dancing on her face. Tess cannot move or take a step. Then the girls and women close in around the table again, and Tess looks at her feet and walks on, beating down the fear.

At the tea they are all looking at her. "What's wrong with you—why don't you answer me?" Evelyn asks her. "Why aren't you eating? And you ate no dinner either. What's wrong? Did you lose your tongue or something?" *I did answer you*, she replies. *I'm not hungry*. But then, after a few more answers, she knows they have not heard her. Her words are not working, the sounds are not coming out of her mouth into the air.

"Did something happen in school, Tess?" Claire asks her softly, and she runs from the kitchen, out to the front hall and up the stairs. At the turn she stands under the stained-glass window. She thinks of the tinker girl's white face. She remembers the day she stuck her tongue out at the tinker girl and now she is dead. She turns her face up to the window, longing for the sun to pour in and warm her. She joins her hands and says a Hail Mary. She listens for the words, to test her sound. But no sound comes. She prays louder, harder. She gives a little cough and tries again. She starts to cry. She touches her face and the feel of the tears makes her cry more. She climbs to the top and runs along the landing to her mother and father's room. From the dressing table she picks up the photograph of her mother in her nurse's uniform and carries it back to her own room. She takes off her boots and gets into bed with the photograph in her hand.

When she wakes it is dark. She knows from the silence of the house that it is the middle of the night. Across the room she can make out Maeve's shape in the other bed. She moves a little and feels the mattress damp under her. She puts a hand down between her legs. She has wet her knickers. She gets out and takes them off and climbs back in, keeping away from the wet spot. She remembers the photograph and feels around until she finds it on the pillow.

Her talk does not come back. Her father and Evelyn bring her down to Dr. O'Beirne, and he sits her up on a high table and asks her questions. But she cannot answer them. One day Denis sits beside her on the low wall. "You'll be all right—any day now you'll be as right as rain," he says. "I bet you by Christmas when Santy comes you'll be talkin' away to him." She says her prayers, like Claire and Mike Connolly tell her to do, but her talk does not come back, not even for Christmas. At school, Mrs. Snee brings her up to her desk and tries, in a kind way, to trick her into talking. On one of her visits Miss Tannian takes her aside, tells her to take deep breaths and say her own name. *Tess*, she keeps saying, *Tess*, as if Tess does not know her own name. Sometimes people get cross with her. She gives up trying to answer them. She looks into all their faces and their eyes and then they give up too. Little by little she gets used to it. She does not miss talking at all. She does everything they ask—all her chores— and they all get used to her silence.

One day when Evelyn and Denis are gone to town her father wants help with the sheep. Tess is told to stand in a gap leading into the yard. Claire is standing at the avenue and Maeve is at the orchard gate, which has fallen off its hinges. Her father and

Mike Connolly go off into the fields to round up the flock. They are gone a long time. Tess hates when there are big jobs like this going on—when the cattle are being dosed, or the sheep are being dipped or shorn. She lies awake at night thinking of all the things that can go wrong, all the dangers.

Then the sheep appear, running, bleating, Captain nipping at their heels, and behind, her father and Mike Connolly. She moves a little to the right, then to the left, trying to spread herself across the gap. She feels the ground shaking from the pounding of their hooves. The smell of them, their greasy wool, reminds her of mutton. Her father shouts, *Keep back a bit*. Mike Connolly is talking to Captain all the time, making little whistling sounds that Captain understands. And then something small and dark— a cat or a rat or a bird—darts across the track and startles Tess and she jumps and one of the sheep sees what Tess has seen and turns and breaks away and rushes towards the gap, towards Tess. The others break and follow and in an instant the whole flock is coming at her, diving past her, right and left, into the open field beyond. Her father and Mike Connolly and Claire are waving their arms, shouting at her. She stands, trapped, as the sheep shoot by, brushing off her arms, leaping past her head, their hooves like thunder so that she has to crouch down and cover her head to save herself.

They are all shouting at her. The sheep are spreading out in the field behind her, Captain after them. They will go on and on through all the gaps into the far fields. Her father is coming, running, his face red. "Get into the house, you!" he roars. "Get in, *get in out of my sight*!" He has his hand raised and she thinks he will lash out and wallop her as he passes. But he runs on in his wellingtons. And then Mike Connolly comes through the gap, older, slower. Their eyes meet for a second. She longs for him to nod or say something, but he looks away and keeps on going.

She walks around to the far side of the house where the sun

never shines and no one ever goes. There's an old rag hanging on the barbed-wire fence. A bird is singing in a tree. She leans over the fence and vomits, her hair falling into the flow. She reaches out for the rag to wipe her mouth. It is her mother's old blouse, faded and tattered, hung out to dry a long time ago, and forgotten.

For a long time she cannot look at her father. She tries to stay out of his path. He has a way of looking at her, a long mean look, as if he is about to say something terrible that will shame her. He keeps his eyes on her when she moves around the kitchen. With each step she is afraid the ground will open and pull her in. She can hardly breathe. *I have no mother*, she thinks, *I have no father*. When he is going to a fair or a funeral, she brings him his good coat and hat. Once, he said, "Good girl," but he never says her name. Mike Connolly says her name. She has grown shy with Mike, and ashamed, since that day with the sheep. Claire is the nicest, always. She says there's a doctor in Dublin who can help her to talk again, but Tess shakes her head. Some nights when the moon shines in her window and shadows cross the wall she jumps out of bed and tiptoes across the landing into Claire and Evelyn's room. Claire puts a finger to her lips and lifts the blankets and lets Tess in beside her. They make chaireens and Tess sleeps all night like that, against Claire's lap, inside Claire's arms.

There are nights when she is afraid to sleep. She lies in her bed, remembering. Captain starts to cry below her window. She gets up and creeps down the stairs and opens the front door. The moonlight is on the steps. She does not say a word, just looks at Captain, and he walks in and follows her up the stairs, into her room. He jumps on the bed and curls up against her. He understands something about her, maybe everything, and her heart begins to open. In the darkness, in the perfect silence, she hears the smallest sounds—Maeve's breath from across the room, the flapping of an insect's wings high up in the corner, the tap dripping far off in the bathroom, and in her mind she sees each drop falling through the air into the white sink, landing and sliding down inside. They are all asleep in their rooms, their eyelids flickering as they dream, and the rooms are silent and sleeping too, and downstairs the coals in the fire are almost gone out but still glow a little in the dark, and a thin line of smoke disappears up the chimney, curling into little puffs along the way. And the table and chairs all stand there, and the dresser, watching, waiting—in her mind she can see them all. And outside, the hens and ducks locked up for the night, and the birds asleep in the trees, and the cows in the cowhouse; and everywhere, all over the farm, worms and insects and small animals are curled up under stones and hedges and bushes. She can see them all. She imagines herself small, so small that she can see everything, hear everything, hear the blades of grass whispering, the pebbles laughing in the dark. She strokes Captain and he sighs. She can feel the beat of his heart against her. She is amazed at how happy she is. In her bed, in this house. With the lawn and the barns and the fields around her. There is nowhere else she wants to be. In her most secret heart she knows there is nowhere she loves more.

When morning breaks she walks outside and crosses the courtyard. It is Saturday and no one is up yet. The sky is blue and the sun has reached the orchard wall. The coach house door is open and inside someone is moving in the shadowy darkness. She looks in and sees Mike Connolly reaching to hang the horse collar up on a hook. When he turns and sees her, he gets a little fright. Then his eyes soften, but he says nothing. A time will come when no one will talk to her at all, or even look at her. She is a disappearing girl.

In the darkness her eye is caught by something bright and shiny on the floor, a coin maybe. She steps inside and as she runs towards it she hits off the corner of the workbench. She cries out. *Ow.* She holds her side and rubs her hip and, when she looks at Mike, the tears come.

"Aw, now, come here to me, *a stór.*" He kneels beside her. He puts an arm around her and makes a pitying sound with his tongue. "Where's it sore?" he asks.

She mumbles through the tears, and keeps rubbing her side. He gets up and goes to where his old coat hangs from a nail and comes back with two toffees. "Now," he says. "Here. Eat this and you'll be better in no time. Sure, you'll be better before you get married!" He takes the paper off and her mouth starts to water. As soon as she tastes the toffee, she smiles.

"Now! What did I tell you, what did I tell you! Of course, now you'll have to marry me!"

It was a game he used to play with herself and Maeve when they were small. Whenever they fell or cut themselves or got upset he'd say, "You'll be better before you get married." She would wipe away the tears and say, "I'm going to marry you when I grow up, Mike."

"I'm going to marry you when I grow up, Mike."

It is the look on his face that tells her he has heard her. She has heard herself too. The sound has come out of her mouth, the words are working. They look at each other. He bites his bottom lip. She holds her breath.

"Well, are you now, Missy!" he says, smiling. "Are you indeed! And who says I'll have you? Hmm? Who says I'll marry you?"

"I say."

"Sure, I might be long married by then. I might have a wife of my own by the time you grow up," he says. "Mmm . . . Unless you marry me now." And he turns and looks around. "Where's the broom at all?"

She had forgotten that part of the wedding game, that the bride and groom have to step over the broom to get married. He walks into the darkness and brings out an old yard brush.

"Now, Missy, I think we're all set. Except for the priest!" He goes outside and lays the brush flat on the gravel. Then he whistles and Captain appears, and he says, *Sit*, and Captain sits still and obedient.

Mike comes and gives her his arm. Through the open door she walks beside him into the winter sun. Captain is there, waiting. Mike begins to hum. She looks up at the sky and hums too and then Mike hums louder as he skips along, almost dancing, with her arm through his. And then they stand before Captain, and Mike tells her what to do, what to say, when to jump over the broom.

"And you too," she says. "You've to jump over the broom too, or else you're not married."

"Oh, I'll jump, I'll jump, to be sure."

"And then will we go and live in your house in Connemara?"

"We will. We'll go and live in Connemara."

And so, standing side by side, they begin. He takes her hand, and bows and says, "Miss Teresa Lohan, do you take me, Michael Joseph Connolly, to be your husband, for better, for worse, in sickness and in health, all the days of our lives?"

Captain cocks his head and whines and she laughs and says, "I do," and jumps over the broom. And then it is her turn.

"Will you, do you, Mike Jophus Connolly, take me, Tess Lohan, as your wife?"

"I do."

He jumps over the broom to her side, and puts his hand in his pocket and brings out hay seeds and chaff and tosses them over their heads. And just as he takes her two hands in his and begins to dance her around the yard, Claire walks out of the house onto the front step and sees them and smiles and comes towards them. Tess waves, calls out, and Claire begins to run, the morning sun on her back.

3 And then, when Tess is ten, there is a real wedding in the house. It is summer again, after a long winter when animals died in the fields and snow fell in May, and Oliver came home. There is something about each day now that she holds dear. Oliver's return for one thing, and something she noticed on those winter nights when she would kneel on her bed and melt a peephole on the frozen windowpane and view everything under snow—the lawn and the trees, the walls and barns and outhouses—all still and beautiful in the moonlight: the feeling that she has grown older and stronger, and safer, and the world has survived and become a little lovelier.

On the morning of Evelyn's wedding Denis drives them all to the church in the new Hillman Minx saloon her father bought that spring. Maeve, who is home from boarding school for the holidays, and Tess are wearing new frocks. In the chapel there are bog asphodels on the altar. The bridegroom sits in the first pew with his brother. It is only the second time that Tess has seen him and he seems to her almost as old as her father.

The wedding breakfast is held at Easterfield. The guests sit at the long table in the dining room. The rations have ended and there is a great spread of food and more talk and laughter in the house than Tess can ever remember. Your mother would be very proud today, someone tells Evelyn. Tess has not given much thought to her mother in recent times. Her face is fading from memory. She tries to picture her mother in these rooms, touching and dusting things, curtains, cushions, softly closing doors. She glances around the room. A feeling sometimes rises in her: the sense of things being alive. When she walks into the coach house or the cowhouse she has the feeling of having just interrupted something. Lately the thought that all the things around her, the things that matter and move her—the trees and fields and animals—have their own lives, their own thoughts, has planted itself in her. If a thing has a life, she thinks, then it has a memory. Memories and traces of her mother must linger all over the house—in rooms and halls and landings. The dent of her feet on a rug. On a cup, the mark of her hand. She wonders if on certain warm nights, when the whole house is sleeping, her mother's soothing self returns, or memories of her return, bringing comfort to things, and promise for their patient waiting. Outside too, the small yard, the fowlhouse—do they miss her? Does the laurel tree remember sheltering her? Tess looks down at her hands. Even as she has these thoughts she knows they are not something she will ever put into words.

After Evelyn's marriage Miss Tannian comes more often, bringing cakes and tarts she has baked, sometimes arriving just before teatime so that she has to be invited to eat with them. She cuts up Oliver's food and butters his bread and tries to wipe his face, before he bats her away. Everyone grows nervous. Tess feels sorry for her. Her father says nothing but frowns often and one evening before they're finished he rises suddenly from the table and storms outside. Later, when Miss Tannian is leaving, Tess sees him cross the courtyard and stand talking to her. Miss Tannian looks flustered and lowers her head and seems to shrink and slide into her car. Many weeks pass before she returns, and when she has finished testing the hens for pinfeathers, she does not linger or enter the house. She rarely visits after that. Once, her father asks, "When was Rose here last?"

It is June and she is in her last week of 6th class, the end of her time in national school. She and Oliver walk home, down the avenue and into the yard. There are men gathered around the old well in the corner. Years ago, long before Tess was born, the well was covered with a flagstone, for fear that the old women from the village who came for water would fall in. For as long as Tess can remember her family has gotten their drinking water from the village pump. On summer evenings the older boys and girls of the village gather there, giddy and tense, something in the air always. One evening her father came over the road and hunted herself and Claire home. "Get home out of that, ye." His face was red with rage. He did not want them mixing. Now the flagstone is pulled away. He will sink his own pump, and men have come to take a sample from the well for testing.

Mike Connolly is holding the end of a rope that snakes down into the darkness. The men edge closer. Her father calls Denis's name. Then he waits. And again, *Denis*. A strange quiet falls on them. Mike Connolly leans over and peers in. She feels fear gathering in the men, a holding of breaths. And then there's a stirring, a shifting of feet and bodies. "He's coming," her father calls. Her father is so full of anger or irritation always, but now his face is open and bright and his voice is full of relief, and for the first time she understands something about his life as a father. She moves closer, sees that there are stone steps descending inside the well, and, as she gazes down, Denis begins to appear out of the darkness. Step by step he climbs, his black head and white face and long thin body rising up out of the well until, pale and dazed, he surfaces and blinks in the sunlight. Mike Connolly puts out a hand, and Denis takes it and steps over the edge onto the gravel. He passes a water bottle to one of the men, his hand shaking. Then, without a word, he turns and crosses the yard.

In September Tess will go, along with Maeve, to the convent boarding school in a town twenty miles away. In the weeks before, preparations are made and new clothes are bought. She has the feeling that these are her last days. She walks around the house and yard, uneasy. She would like her father to notice her, to acknowledge that she is leaving. Just once, she would like to please him.

At the school she is accompanied everywhere by the peal of bells, the smell of wax, and the echo of her feet on polished floors. A feeling of melancholy registers when the strains of hymn singing waft out from the chapel. In the classroom teachers in gowns stand on the raised dais, and some, with just a word or a hand on a book, hint of things to come, of a wider world that gives her a feeling of lift and light and promise. At night in the dormitory the sound of forty sleeping girls commingles with thoughts of home and Oliver and Claire and her father, and Denis, in his silence. Some nights she cries. She would like to have taken them all with her, make them all fit into her new world. So this is homesickness, she thinks. But there is something about the pitch of her pain that is not all terrible. There is something true and clear and cleansing about it that makes her want to endure it. It is a test, a wall she must break through. She takes comfort in knowing that Maeve is there, that somewhere in the building there is one who shares her blood and knows everything of her life before now.

She is fond of all subjects, except Mathematics—algebra, trigonometry with its baffling formulae—and does well in her exams. But she is wary, watchful all the time. Only in English class when the teacher recites Wordsworth or John Donne does she briefly forget where she is, carried by sound and image to faraway villages and rivers, and cathedrals rising to meet the heavens. At these moments she has the feeling that there is something at hand, that she is coming close to something she cannot quite reach, but which she knows is right and beautiful. She does not like to speak in class, and on the rare occasions when she is required to answer a question or recite a poem, her insides contract, and she is rigid with fear that she will say something foolish and shame herself. When it is her turn to read, the teachers merely nod to her. She is certain that not one of them knows her name.

She grows to love the school chapel with its sanctuary lamp and stained-glass windows. On Sundays and holy days—All Souls, Holy Week, Pentecost—the priest reads from the Scriptures, the Psalms, with a lilting voice, the Latin words pouring over her, more easily understood now. *Dominus vobiscum. Et cum spiritu tuo.* The swing of the thurible at Benediction and the smell of incense, the peal of little bells. But it is the choir—the clear pristine voices and the somber notes rising from the organ—that stirs something deep in her. *Panis Angelicus. Tantum Ergo. O Salutaris Hostia.*

In her second year her Latin teacher falls ill and a new teacher, Mr. Brown, temporarily takes her place. He is tall, gray-haired, and does not wear the black gown that the other teachers wear. Though he lives in the town, he speaks with a scholarly accent—perhaps even English. His voice is soft. She notices the kind way he has of listening—how when a girl is answering a question he does not look directly at her, yet fully attends. One day at the end of class he singles Tess out and asks her to wait back.

She stands before him.

"I see that you're from my part of the county, Miss Lohan," he says. "On the school roll, your address caught my eye."

Her heart takes fright. A raft of fears passes through her: he knows her father; her father has not paid the school fees; she is here under false pretenses. She is an imposter.

He looks out over his glasses at her, and waits. She does not know what he expects. He sits back, takes off his glasses.

"I was born in Easterfield House," he says, and pauses. "I lived there until I was eight. My family sold the place, and then a few years later your father bought the house and some of the land."

She is lost for words. She has never given thought to Easterfield's past. She cannot conceive of this man in its rooms, its beds, running through the fields.

"How is the old house?" He is smiling, as if asking after a relative.

"It's good, sir."

"Does the roof still leak? Every so often rainwater would collect in the valley and burst through the ceiling."

"Yes, sir, that happened once, when I was small. The ceilings upstairs were ruined. I don't remember it, but the stains are still there."

"And your father farms the land? Livestock?"

"Yes, sir."

"And you have brothers and sisters? A brother, who will inherit the place perhaps?"

"Yes, sir. Denis, my older brother."

He looks at her for what seems a long time. She thinks he is about to announce a visit to Easterfield. He will take her in his car tomorrow and they will arrive, with no forewarning. She starts to panic.

"It is quite something, coming on you like this." He looks away and is quiet for a moment. "Do you know of Easterfield's history? Do you know when the house was built?"

"Yes, sir. My old teacher said it was built in 1678."

She remembers the day in 5th class when Mr. Clarke stopped in the middle of a History lesson and told her to stand and tell the class about Easterfield. She was mortified. Her father had bought the house and a hundred acres in 1911, she said in a low voice, and her parents got married in 1925. She did not say that her mother had once told her that the house had three hundred and sixty-five windows, a window for every day of the year. It was not true; she counted them once and got only thirty-seven. "We have an orchard, and two stairs," she said, and could think of no more.

"Is that it? Is that all you know? Sit down, Tess Lohan," Mr. Clarke said, and then looked around the class before continuing.

"Easterfield House and estate was owned by the Cannon family from 1678 until the 1800s. King Charles the Second granted them five hundred acres. The house was closed up in the 1830s but was reopened as a famine hospital to treat the sick and the starving during the 1840s. The locals." He paused, and looked into individual children's eyes. Tess had feared he would alight on her again.

Now Mr. Brown reaches into his bag, brings out a book.

"You know then that the house was used as a hospital during the Famine?"

"Yes, sir."

"And that hundreds of patients died there? I only discovered this myself relatively recently. A few years ago I compiled a history of all the big houses and estates in the area. I was quite shocked by what I found out about Easterfield. The unclaimed corpses were buried on the land. In the ditches, down in the quarry, under trees—the groves of oak and beech—anywhere. Places that I remember, where I'd played . . . They threw lime on the bodies to prevent the stench."

He grows thoughtful. "My family did not come into possession of Easterfield until some time later. They were, I believe, kind to the tenants."

Tess nods. All she wants now is to leave. He hands her the book. "Perhaps you'd like to borrow this. Bring it back tomorrow."

Later, in bed, she remembers talk at school and at the village pump about local people who claimed to have heard the cries of the dead when they passed Easterfield at night. She remembers the rope swing that Denis hung from a tree above the quarry for herself and Oliver, and their laughter as they swung out high over the rocks. In her mind she moves through the farm, remembering each field, each copse of trees. She sees the boughs, bare in winter. She feels a chill and pulls the bedclothes tight around her and tries to sleep.

4 After three years, Tess's schooling comes to an abrupt end. Maeve has gone to train as a teacher at Carysfort Training College in Dublin and money is scarce. But that is not all. During the summer Tess spends six weeks away from home, helping Evelyn following the birth of her third child. From the strain of housework and care of Evelyn's babies she is tired all the time. By nightfall she is weak and every breath she takes is a painful stab. She develops a cough which so alarms Evelyn that the doctor is summoned.

It is not mentioned, TB, but it is what everyone fears. At the convent, girls would mysteriously disappear, to return six months later, or not at all. Though it has never been said, it is, she suspects, what caused her mother's death. It is why her mother's room was fumigated and why they were all tested.

She has pleurisy, not TB. Nevertheless she must spend three months in the fever hospital in Galway. Her spirits sink when she enters the ward of thin pale-faced women. She settles into her bed and looks out at the windless day, time stretching before her. A flock of starlings rises and blackens the sky. A memory of home, and then of school, materializes. At that moment she understands and begins to mourn what is lost. Exhausted, she lies down and looks up at the ceiling, waiting for her lungs to dry up and quieten. Later, rested, she seeks out books. The hospital library consists of two shelves of ancient-looking paperbacks at the end of a corridor. *The Lives of the Saints*, *Romeo and Juliet*, *The Red and the Black*, *The World of Plants*. She reads them all. She counts the days until Denis and Claire and her father come to visit. Then, when they come, there is not much said and the visit is soon over. When they leave she stands at the window looking down at patients shuffling around the grounds.

The patients are mainly from the city. But there is one boy, Tony, a shy loping teenager—almost a man—who is from the country. He is tall—nearly too tall—and hangs his head and has large agricultural hands. She feels a pull to him and senses his pull too, and more and more her thoughts turn to him. But then one evening something happens: a commotion arises at the back of the common room. A woman squeals. There is a rat. She catches a glimpse of the thing with a long brown-and-white body—like the piebald horse the tinkers keep—and a tail as long as the body and a belly that grazes the floor, darting along, disappearing into a hole in the corner. Tony—his eyes wild—is lunging after it, intent, and then he bends and inserts his long middle finger into the hole after the rat. Again and again, he thrusts his finger in to the hilt, poking, jiggling it around, frantically trying to get at the rat.

On her return home, she slips back into life at Easterfield, into the rounds of housework and the comings and goings on the farm, under the roof with her father and brothers and Claire, and Mike Connolly. Though she herself does not feel delicate, the word attaches to her, and she is spared from heavy tasks and farm work. She begins to mark events—the births of Evelyn's children, Oliver leaving the national school, her father's £200 win on the Sweepstakes, the arrival of electricity. In the dark corner under the back stairs she writes these dates on the distempered wall. When she is eighteen Denis teaches her to drive, and, from then on she regularly drives her father to fairs and funerals. One hot summer's day, with Maeve home on holidays from her teaching job in Dublin, they drive their father to the sheep fair in the town, leaving him to his business among the pens and carts and dealers. They browse the shops for an hour, and then, flushed and giddy and parched with the thirst, they enter the hotel in the square. In the carpeted lounge off the hall they stand at the bar and order two glasses of orange and then turn to find their father sitting with a group of men in the corner, talking and drinking and haggling over prices. When he sees them his face darkens. He does not acknowledge them, or even glance at them later when they leave. On the way home his fuming silence fills the car. Inside the house, he breaks out. They have no shame entering a public bar like that, sitting up on high stools with men watching them. Like streetwalkers. Laughing and streecing and making a show of themselves. Making a show of him. "How is it at all that things are always going against me?"

He is full of aggravation. They have learned not to respond to his barging, his oppressive silence, his sighing. They have each, in their separate ways, learned how to read him, how to evade his wrath, how to gauge when his guard is down and they might seek advantage. Over the summer the three sisters, with Denis at the wheel, drive to dances organized by the Pioneer Association or the Ploughing Association and to carnivals held in marquees in local towns. Always, the next morning there is an inquisition. *Who did ye meet? Who did ye talk to? Were the Burkes there?* Tess lets the others answer. She remembers the men lined up on one side of the dance floor and the women on the other. She danced with every man who asked her, not because she wished to, but because she sensed something of the dread that these hopeful anxious men had endured just to ask, and the awful humiliation they would suffer if she refused.

Out of the blue, a letter arrives from their mother's sister Molly, in America, inviting Claire to come out. At first Tess thinks it is a holiday invitation. But the word and the image of the place, *America*, evoke a feeling of exile and eternal loneliness. In the weeks following, as the practicalities are worked out—Molly secures a job for Claire at the Bell Telephone Company, where she herself works—and the departure date is set, a feeling of dread falls on Tess.

She does not go with Denis and Oliver and their father to see Claire off at Cobh. She does not want to possess a memory of that parting. The feeling that everything good in her life is now vanishing is too much to bear. She sits in the quiet of the house all morning. She takes down notepaper and envelopes and writes to the only two hospitals in Dublin whose names she has ever heard of. In neat handwriting she states her eagerness to train as a nurse. She gives details of her education and asserts her suitability for the profession. *My late mother was a nurse and I would like to continue the family tradition in this vocation.*

A month before her twentieth birthday she receives a letter from the Mater Hospital offering her a place as a trainee nurse, pending an interview, character references, and the payment of a fee. On a September morning she boards the train at Woodlawn Station and is ferried across the country, into the unknown. Somewhere in the midlands the sky darkens and the train slows to a halt in the middle of nowhere. There is an eerie silence in the carriage. Suddenly a fork of lightning cuts the sky in two. With her heart crossways she watches the lighted sky as each angry flash erupts and dazzles and disappears.

She resides in the Nurses' Home among other girls from the country. Every morning she dons her starched uniform and white shoes and goes on duty. In the evenings she attends classes. She is eager, and learns quickly, in both theory and practice. At night she sits on her bed poring over her textbooks, occasionally startled by a siren in the streets outside. She writes to her father every fortnight and to Claire in New York almost every week. On her days off she walks along O'Connell Street, gazing in shop windows, occasionally entering Clerys to buy nylons or a cardigan and once, during their winter sale, a herringbone tweed coat with a fur collar and cuffs. She goes to the cinema with a girl from Cork, but mostly avoids social gatherings and nights out. The shyness she feels among others and the terrible need to fit in cause her such anxiety that when the evening arrives the prospect of going among people renders her immobile, disabled, sometimes physically sick. Whenever possible, she opts for night duty, the low lights and the hush of the ward offering the closest thing to solitude available in a working life. When she meets the gaze of an attractive young doctor at a patient's bedside she blushes and averts her eyes, longing to respond with a flirtatious smile or remark, like the other girls do. She joins the library at Phibsborough, borrows two novels each week, goes for walks along the city streets and down by the river. One day, on Townsend Street, she stands at the entrance to a new building that houses a swimming pool and reads a notice for swimming classes. She has an image of herself cutting a swathe, a solitary furrow, through still blue water. During the two years of her training, and afterwards as a ward nurse, she is warm and polite with her colleagues, but fails to form one lasting friendship.

Occasionally, on a Saturday when she is off duty, she meets

up with Maeve, in from her digs in Blackrock, and the two sisters stroll around the city. Once, in February, as they walk along the footpath outside the GPO, a street photographer appears before them and takes their picture. They are walking arm in arm, both in fashionable tweed coats and pointed black shoes. Later when Tess looks at herself in the photograph she sees for the first time what others must see—a young woman with a nice enough face and smiling eyes—something that does not accord with the image of herself she carries within. She places the photograph in an envelope and writes a note and addresses it to Claire, care of her aunt Molly's, 731 West 183rd Street, New York. She looks at the address for a long time. *183rd Street.* She says it aloud. She sees Claire there, sitting in a chair. She feels something, a streaming across, at that moment.

With each trip back to Easterfield, changes accrue. Captain is gone. He slunk from the shadows on his belly one day and lay under the wheel of the car as it entered the yard. Often, she replays this image in her mind and remembers his small black eyes gazing into hers on those nights when she took him up to her room. Mike Connolly returned to his own people in Connemara, too old and ill now—and no longer needed—to endure the labor or fulfill the duties he had performed at Easterfield for nearly thirty-five years.

Oliver, more than anyone, has changed. He is tall and handsome with a shock of blond hair and mischievous blue eyes—so different from Denis's dark brooding looks. You will charm the birds in the trees, she tells him. And your beauty will cast a spell, she thinks. He has learned to drive. He takes the car out at night to pubs and dances, indicating a certain wildness of character that is not ordinarily tolerated in Easterfield but to which, somehow, her father turns a blind eye. Tess slips into her old ways with her father when she is back—an attitude of reverence, obedient service, meekness. She has seen him age. One night in the kitchen a memory surfaces. It is, she thinks, her first memory of him. She is no more than two or three years old and she is in his arms, being lifted high onto the back of a horse. She is terrified and starts to cry, and he lifts her down, then holds her against his warm face.

A peaceful lull falls on the kitchen, and she looks at him. "Will I cut your hair?" she asks. He turns his head towards her, and she waits to be denounced. He looks at her, baffled, stunned, as if he has suddenly found himself somewhere else. His chin begins to quiver, and he looks down. She is flooded with tender feelings for him. She sees for the first time all he has endured. Holding things together, holding himself together, poised, always, to defend against a new catastrophe. She gets up and lays a towel on his shoulders and begins to cut his hair. Neither of them says a word. She is moved by his silent acquiescence. Gently she takes each strand and cuts, the sound of the scissors in the air between them, the hair falling to the floor. And his sorrow, for all that is lost, lying silent within him.

Part Two

5 Late in the summer of '62 Tess flew on a TWA flight from Shannon Airport to New York. Before she left that morning her father handed her a £50 note, and then shook her hand formally, awkwardly. Denis and Maeve, and Evelyn in a hat and pregnant again, sat into the car. As they drove away Tess looked back at the house, her eyes lingering on the upstairs windows, then out at the land. Halfway down the avenue, Denis stopped the car to get something from the boot. She turned her head to the lone ash tree among the beeches and saw, for the first time, a band of barbed wire embedded in the trunk, the flesh forced to grow over the spikes in pained little folds and swellings. Denis sat in and they drove on. How had she missed this before? Who had done it? This was Lohan land, a Lohan tree. So, a Lohan hand.

At the airport the summer wind gusted and blew Evelyn's hat off and she ran after it, and they all laughed. This will be my memory, she thought. As they parted, they threw holy water on her and she blessed herself. Denis looked down, his long arms hanging, and she remembered the injured ash again.

Before the takeoff, she grew frantic. The plane roared down the runway and she bent her head. It was not flying she feared, but dying. When the wheels lifted and the plane began to climb she pressed her fingers to her ears. Then she remembered the date: August fifteenth, the Feast of the Assumption of Our Lady into Heaven, and her heart began to quell. God would not let a plane crash on Our Lady's feast day. She began to fill up with trust, like a child newly assured. The roar of the engine eased and the plane leveled and in a while she opened her eyes. They were in upper Earth. They had broken through into the blue. Dazzling light. Glorious. For a moment all thoughts ceased and there was this: a glimpse, a proximity, a feeling of being a fraction of a second away from something pure and sublime, a hairsbreadth from the divine. And then it was gone, the clarity, the fleeting elation, and she looked up and saw the other passengers sitting there reading, sleeping, or in quiet contemplation.

Claire's husband, Peter, a tall handsome Irish-American, was waiting at Idlewild Airport. Shyly she climbed into his car and he whisked her up to Peekskill on the Hudson, where they had taken a summer house. Everything was different—the highway, the sky, the distant forests. The vast country, green and clean and perfect. The trucks thundering past with huge chrome wheels and invisible drivers high up in cabs. For a while she forgot where she was. The trees are juniper, Peter said. His teeth were white and gleaming. Juniper, she said to herself. Beautiful word, beautiful trees. They stopped at a turnpike and paid a toll, just to use the road.

There, on the front lawn of a low-slung villa above the river, stood Claire, a small child at her feet, another one inside her. Unable to utter a word, they embraced. When they drew away, there were tears in each other's eyes. Their aunt Molly was there, up from the city to welcome Tess, a large buoyant woman with a shock of white frizzy hair. They moved to the backyard. Later, Peter's extended family came by and he lit the barbecue and poured drinks and everyone milled around the pool. Outside, on the street, big American cars floated by. In the hours and days that followed, Tess would sometimes look around at the kids and the cars and the pool, at the picture windows and the sun-drenched world she had tumbled into. Once or twice she remembered home, Evelyn's hat and the injured ash. And then forgot them. In the evening the crickets sang. Peter came up behind Claire, stroked her back, gazed tenderly at her swollen belly. This is what he has done to her, Tess thought. This act of love, of sex, on her sister. In a book, once, she had come on the words *fruit of my loins*. She remembered the nights she had climbed into Claire's bed and slept in her arms. They looked at each other now. In the look was an acknowledgment, a declaration, an affirmation that everything was finally settled, and the lives being lived here were the right ones, the ideal lives.

Slowly, in the months that followed, Tess tuned to the frequency of the city, to the accents and the street grid and the subway, to the black faces on the sidewalk, the sirens at night, the five-and-ten-cent stores teeming with goods, and buildings that rose up daily from gaps in the streets. The new words too— *pocketbook, meat loaf, lima beans, Jell-O*. The taste of coffee, the clothes so lovely and cheap and slim-fitting. The abundance of everything.

In September she started work at the Presbyterian Medical Center on East 68th Street, and in the early weeks walked the long corridors every day shadowing her seniors, pushing medicine carts, taking blood, listening, learning, delivering all that was expected of her as things came at her, and her heart beat hard. Unconsciously, she adjusted her accent to be understood, and altered her handwriting until it attained the grace and slant of American script. She sat by herself in the cafeteria. The pall of loneliness that accompanied her from her aunt's apartment each morning, and which was briefly eclipsed by her duties, lowered itself again. At night in the apartment she studied for her nursing accreditation or sat in the living room with Molly and

Molly's other boarder—a German man in his sixties, named Fritz—with the fan whirring and *I Love Lucy* or *The Jack Paar Show* on TV. When the audience laughed, she felt herself apart, among strangers. Exhausted, homesick, she went to bed and recited the Rosary and afterwards lay tense and sleepless for a long time under a cotton sheet. She woke after what seemed like mere minutes to the squeal of a garbage truck on the street below and the vague anxiety that she always experienced at dawn brimming up again.

Fritz was a machinist in a factory downtown. In the apartment he fetched and fixed things, and on Fridays he carried home the shopping from the Safeway store on 183rd Street. On Saturday nights he and Molly sat in the living room, drinking—he, small shots, she, highballs of whiskey. On weekday evenings all three of them sat at the table and ate pot roast or ham steak and sweet potato. Afterwards Fritz and Tess washed up, and then Fritz tuned the radio to a jazz station for the night. One night as he turned the dial she caught a snatch of a song she recognized and, in its beat, briefly forgot herself, until she became aware of Fritz's eyes on her. The next evening he came in and handed her a box. "This is for you," he said, in his sad accent. Inside was a new transistor radio. The kettle on the stove began to sing. She saw the jets of flame underneath, their fragile blue beauty, and when she looked up at Fritz she was overcome by a memory of home and Mike Connolly.

One Saturday they rode a bus across the George Washington Bridge out to New Jersey for the christening of Claire's new baby. Fritz carried bags with containers of fried chicken and bean salad and beer. Tess brought gifts for Claire's little boy, Patrick, and the new baby, Elizabeth, named after their mother. Peter met them at the bus station and drove them to a street of houses with verandas and driveways and sloping lawns, the kind that had become familiar to Tess from TV.

Molly and Fritz took charge of the kitchen. Claire took Tess upstairs to see the new baby. The sight of the child moved her. She thought her a miracle. Out of Claire she had come, from Claire's flesh and blood. So close to Tess's own biology, the same blood coursing through her veins. The blood that binds us all, she thought, now and in the past. She looked down at the child, at the closed eyes. A clean slate, pure and unblemished. Not long born, not long out of the other realm.

There was a little whimper and then a cry, and Claire lifted the child and began to nurse her. Tess went to leave but Claire whispered to stay. The blinds were down and a small lamp cast a pink glow in the room. She caught sight of Claire's bare white breast and the engorged nipple directed into the child's mouth.

"I have to tell you something," Claire said. She did not look up. "We're moving to California. Peter's being transferred out there."

There were footsteps on the landing, a child's voice. Patrick pushed open the door. "You'll come out and visit us, won't you?" Her hand, as she reached out to touch her son's head, was trembling.

They drove to the church for the christening. In the afternoon, guests filled the house, the children running around. The adults mingled in the open-plan rooms and spilled out into the backyard. At dusk they were getting a little drunk, laughing, leaning against walls. Tess stood apart, sipping a beer, keeping an eye on the pool, the children. She looked at her watch, added five hours. A map of America came to mind, the West Coast, images from TV of wagon trains crossing wide-open plains. Peter was talking to two men and a young woman, work colleagues. He was smoking a cigarette, holding a glass of wine. He leaned and bumped softly against the woman, and said something. The garden lights came on. Tess moved to a quiet corner. There were earthquakes in California. Her father's brother had gone there years ago and never returned.

The young woman moved away from Peter, drifted in and out of other groups, touching men's arms. Claire came out and stood with Tess, smiling. She seemed smaller, thinner. Then her eyes moved off and her smile waned. Tess turned and watched Peter stride across the yard and in one swift wordless movement he picked up the young woman and threw her in the pool.

In the city she felt the stir of anxiety on the streets, and day by day it entered her. On the TV, missiles, warheads, ships steaming towards Cuba. The end of the world. Fritz sat quiet and somber. In the mornings she felt the foreboding, the impending doom, gigantic explosions and firestorms flashing across her mind. She thought of home, her father, Evelyn in a houseful of kids, danger floating close. No one was safe. One day she saw a rich woman emerge from a building, usher children into a taxi. Everywhere an exodus, people holding their breath, looking at one another. As if we are all brothers and sisters, Tess thought. One night the president addressed the nation. She was mesmerized by his beauty, his pain, as if the words themselves afflicted him. *Thank you and good night.*

And then the ships turned back. *We were all brought together in fear and mutual need*, she wrote to her father, *and now its passing has brought something else—hope, love—down on the streets.* She had found a new language—this country had given her new ways to think and speak. One Saturday afternoon Fritz took her up to Loew's Paradise Theatre in the Bronx. In the foyer was a fountain of Italian marble and, all over the walls, murals and hanging vines. In the dark theater she sat deep in a velvet seat and when she looked up there was a moonlit sky above her, and stars twinkling and clouds passing by. A week later she returned to the Bronx and bought five dresses in a dress store, one lovelier than the other, because she could. She took the subway back down to 181st Street and walked out into the autumn sun and floated along the sidewalk, catching herself for a moment in that concentrated life.

6 Month by month in that first year Tess discovered a rhythm to her life in the city. The early-morning rise, the subway ride downtown, the day spent among patients and colleagues on the ward. On Sundays when she was off duty, she went to Mass with her aunt Molly at the chapel of St. Elizabeth's Hospital. On other days she went to the library on West 179th Street and browsed the bookshelves and sat at a table reading. She came to understand that she could live almost anywhere, so long as there was someone of hers—her own kin—there. Claire had moved to San Francisco earlier in the year. Still, she is in the country, she thought, she is in the same land.

Occasionally, she went shopping or up to a *céilí* in Gaelic Park in the Bronx with other Irish nurses. She longed to give herself up to their good cheer and lightness. Being among people left her feeling lonely, even, at times, endangered. She felt divided from others. Their talk, their dreams, seemed to her incidental, artificial, something that had to be got through en route to the real conversation, the heart of the matter. She found herself waiting for someone who shared her sensations. One day, at a patient's bedside, at a tender moment approaching death, she looked into the attending physician's eyes and he looked into hers and she felt an affinity with him. It was this she craved. She had had intimations of it in books. Perhaps such things, even such people, existed only in books. She was reading *Dr. Zhivago* then. She sat in a corner of the cafeteria at lunchtime, transported. She was Lara in the battlefield hospital. She was lost to Yuri. She journeyed in the snow, felt their grief. Sometimes she cried. The feelings called to mind moments from childhood, when she was distant from herself but experienced the same peace, as if she were entering another dimension, one that contained the answer to a question she could not yet form. She looked up from her book. Though she felt sure it existed, she was not sure such knowledge could be attained or recovered. Or at least not by her. She did not even know what the question was, aware only of vague intimations. Such knowledge was beyond her, requiring more intelligence or learning, or a higher faculty of feeling, than she possessed. At this realization she grew dispirited. She rose from the table and went down in the elevator and returned to the bustle of the ward, to the clanking of carts and bedpans and the humming of machines.

In early spring she transferred to the 168th Street campus of the hospital and to the private wing, the Harkness Pavilion. There she befriended another Irish nurse, Anne Beckett from Wexford, who had come out several years before and was now engaged to be married. Together they went to the St. Patrick's Day Parade on Fifth Avenue, and just before Easter they rented an apartment, a fifth-floor walk-up, at 471 Academy Street in Inwood. It was unfurnished except for a single bed in each bedroom. They bought a table, four chairs, and a sofa from a couple upstairs. They bought delph and pots and pans, and brightly colored curtains for the bedrooms. They shared evening meals at the kitchen table and Anne told her about the movie stars and singers who had been patients. Marilyn Monroe had been in the psychiatric wing, though Anne had not nursed her. She had nursed Elizabeth Taylor and Mrs. Roosevelt and Cole Porter, who had a maimed leg that he named Geraldine.

Tess wrote to Oliver. *Oh, Oliver, you have to come out. There's room now at Aunt Molly's. I think about you and Denis and Dadda a lot. And Dadda's terrible moods, and his silence. I doubt he will ever change. Maybe Easterfield does that, makes everyone silent. There's nothing for you there, Oliver. You can be anyone here. Anything you dream of. How is Denis? Poor Denis . . . I miss you all. I dreamt of Mike Connolly the other night. He was standing by the old well in the yard. Do you remember that time Dadda sank the pump, Oliver? Denis climbed down for a sample and Mike held the rope . . .*

One Sunday morning in May she woke to the sound of talk and laughter in the kitchen. Anne had come off night duty and Tim, her fiancé, was there, and Anne's brother and other boys who had recently come out from Ireland. They were frying eggs and waffles. When she entered the kitchen and saw them around the table, she was reminded of summer evenings in Easterfield long ago when the tea was being readied and the wireless was on, before the silence took hold. The radio was on now too, the baseball scores being read in a beautiful melliferous voice, but they were hardly listening, full of their own talk. Their familiar accents pleased her. A shy boy from Kerry got up and gave her his chair, moved away with his plate of eggs. She looked around at their open happy faces and sat among them.

Later they left for the park, urging her to follow. She sat among the dishes, the day stretching before her. She looked at the egg stains on the plates, the empty mugs, the chairs pushed back. Something of the others still drifted there. The sun shone in the window and fell on the pot of marmalade, on the chunky orange peel inside.

She walked the few blocks to Broadway. Up ahead she saw the trees of Inwood Hill Park. She turned left, entered the library at Broadway and Dyckman, its hush and concentrated silence bringing contentment. On a table a large art book lay open. She turned the pages, dazzled by the colors, the yellows and oranges and blues, their intensity. A street café at night. A strange simple bedroom that exerted a lure, a childish longing. A cornfield with crows that made her heart collapse. She stared at the field and the crows, sad and familiar. She began to read. The artist had cut off his own ear, died by his own hand. She turned each page. Letters to his brother. The kindness of Theo moved her. And the life, the words . . .

I always have the impression of being a traveler going somewhere, to some destination . . . I feel in myself a fire . . . the passersby just see a little smoke . . . I know that I could be an utterly different man. There is something inside me.

Walking along the street, for no reason, she began to cry. She tried to focus on her footsteps, beat a rhythm between each tree. When her tears passed, she saw things clearly. Each person's face, the nose and eyes, the buttons on their shirts, the shivery pattern of leaves. Beauty everywhere. After a little distance a space began to open inside her, the aftermath of pain. She stood on the sidewalk, as in a dream. Silence. Light. She was ready to be transformed.

She entered the park in late afternoon. Across the green she saw them, sprawled on a gentle slope before a blazing flower bed, laughing, smoking, the group larger now. She was approaching along the path from the north. She saw him instantly, a stranger, a little apart. Long, lean, blond. He was talking to Tim and when she came close he looked up and fell silent and she felt a powerful signal. In the minutes that followed he did not look at her once, and she could not bear to look at him either.

His name was David. He was a cousin of Anne's, out from

Dublin, working for the last nine months with a firm of lawyers in Midtown. He reminded her of a brighter, quieter Oliver.

Later, she found herself sitting beside him. He reached out a hand and passed her a soda. She saw he was a *citóg* and watched him closely after that. He had been to university. She felt inferior, always, among city people, among the educated. He spoke with a city accent. She became acutely aware of her own. She told him she had trained in the Mater Hospital.

"I grew up in Glasnevin, not far from the Mater," he said. He smiled at her. She told him she used to visit the Botanic Gardens on her days off. She saw a monkey puzzle tree there. She had never heard of a monkey puzzle tree before that.

"The Gardens are just around the corner from my home," he said. They might have passed each other on the street. He was silent then, as if reconsidering what he was about to say. His arms were tanned, with a thick crop of gold hairs.

"When I was ten," he said, "I saw a tree there struck by lightning. I was with my brother. It went up in flames in front of us. I was terrified, rooted to the spot . . . but under a sort of spell too."

She told him about her work, her home, the little groves of oak and beech. His legs were long, strong, muscular. The sight of them made her shy.

"I have an uncle, a teacher, in Australia," he said. "He told me in a letter once that in the bush, years ago, when the police were hunting down outlaws like Ned Kelly, they'd burn a tree to keep warm on cold nights. They'd find a dead tree and set it alight there where it stood, and gather around it. Then the outlaws would see the burning tree in the distance and make off, gaining ground through the night."

He had beautiful hands. He was so far from Denis and Oliver, his life so polished, that she felt a pang of pity for them, for all they lacked. At this thought she felt suddenly disloyal.

"Do you like it here, in New York?" she asked.

He looked out across the park. "Yes, I suppose. I don't like the evenings. Late summer evenings when . . ."

He did not finish. He took out cigarettes and offered her one. She shook her head. He lit his own and exhaled. She was aware of every breath, the flex of every muscle, where his eyes fell, his hands. To be this watchful, this attuned to a man, a stranger, excited and confused her. He lit another cigarette and looked pensive. He was on the point of telling her something else, but he stood up and moved away, and she felt the parting like a loss.

Later, when they drew near again, he did not say much. He gave off an air of mild irritation, as if regretting all he had told her. Then a silence, a pall, began to envelop them. It took all her talk away.

7 From a distance he exerted a great force on her. She craved solitude to conjure him up again, finding significance only in the recall of that day. Everything moved her. Every sight and sound, every song, every man's face—the whole city—turned him over to her. She went out to Brooklyn one morning with Anne to help choose Anne's trousseau. In the afternoon they left the shops, each enwrapped in her own fantasy. They walked along a street with a slight incline where kids rode bikes along the cracked pavement, calling out to one another in the bright sun. She gazed at the clapboard houses and imagined the backyards and clotheslines and husbands sitting in the shade. She began to imagine coming home to this, entering, calling out "I'm home, honey," and he in the kitchen peeling onions, frying meat. The meat browning on the pan, the smells, the sounds of the kitchen. She, pausing in the hall, hearing the children outside, breathing deeply before entering the kitchen, then standing behind him, laying her face against his back. Home. She shook herself out of the reverie and smiled at Anne. They rode the subway back into the city, trundling along under the hot streets into the heart of Manhattan.

———

Oliver came out in June and found work in construction. The American sun bleached him blonder. On weekends he joined Tess and Anne and their social group. They went out to New Jersey for a Fourth of July garden party. Oliver was handsome beyond words. His blue-eyed charm reminded her of the Kennedys. If you weren't my brother, she thought, I'd marry you. There was no one to whom she felt closer than to her siblings, no greater bond. She thought of David constantly. Already he had forgotten her. She felt the approach of hurt. She tried to glean things from Anne, careful not to betray the tug she felt. The longing to see him became a kind of sickness.

And then, one Saturday, there he was, on the beach at Coney Island when they arrived. Sitting on a towel in their crowded patch near the water, smoke trailing from his fingers. Emblazoned in the sun, the glittering sea before him. He looked up, wordless, unyielding. But something in his eyes—a flash, a shock—before he averted them, and she knew she had not been wrong, that what she had felt was the truth. She retreated, and watched him from a safe distance. When he removed his shirt she saw his chest, his skin, his bare beauty. She thought of a deer, stark, sleek, nervy. Now and then he looked out at the ocean with a far-off gaze. In an instant he could break her heart.

All day long, they came and went, swimming and eating and talking. She stayed close to Oliver. She looked at the others, wondering at their lives now, their mothers and fathers back home. All the time the sea, the wing flash of gulls, him on the edge of her vision. She had to pass him to get to the water, and she half ran, shy, feeling the pull, the oscillation in him: in a glance, an invitation, in the next, a rejection. *Admit it*, she wanted to cry. *Only the truth matters.* Tense, febrile, she threw herself on her towel and watched him through half-closed eyes in a swirl of sun and cigarette smoke. A birthday card was passed around and he took the pen in his left hand and tilted his head and half twisted his torso and hooked his wrist at an awkward painful angle, and scratched out the words. She was rooted to the spot. In his hooked hand, his twisted body, she saw a striving, something that rendered him vulnerable. Misshapen hand, she thought, misshapen words. Misshapen man. The effort implied something fragile, broken, a wound far greater than any visible deformity.

The sun beat down. From the promenade, the cries of carousel riders carried in the air. She got up, walked into the water, pushed her legs against the weight of the sea. She had learned to swim in Dublin, the one thing in her life that she had ever mastered. Chest-high in the waves she lowered her head, raised her legs, let her body float, the ocean under her. She lay on the shimmering surface. The swell of each wave lifted her, then gently lowered her again. She was almost dreaming, the sun on her back.

And then he was there, gliding silently under her. Hair flowing back from his temples, his head pushing on. All sound muted by water. She glided, opened her arms and legs, swam parallel above him. They were beyond the reach of others, moving in perfect unison, two sea creatures, cold, radiant, luminous. They swam further, deeper, through sudden patches of cold. She had an urge to wrap her legs around him, ride on his back down into the dark.

And then he banked and they were before each other in the underwater silence. His eyes blinked, searched hers. He brought a hand to her face, stroked it. Air bubbles rose from his mouth. A faint frown, and then a smile. She was elated. And then he was gone, surging upwards, breaking the surface into sunlight. In his after-tow she lost her tread and floundered for a second and lunged back towards the shore, desperate for the touch of the sea floor.

In the evening, they gathered up their belongings and piled onto the boardwalk, to the hot dog and drinks stands. Oliver and the others drifted off. They found themselves together again, a sphere of uncalm surrounding them. His silence was overbearing, a force field, sucking everything out of her. He raised his head and looked from him, as if nothing had happened. There was an eerie depth to him, an inwardness that was infinite. She thought he was not in command of it.

That night they all met up again at City Center ballroom on West 55th Street. She was fevered, agitated, consumed by the day's events. The ballroom was heaving, dancers jiving to the Irish show band. Oliver found a raven-haired girl and never left her side. Anne and Tim danced and then, pitying her, Anne went to the bathroom and Tim took her onto the floor. The crowd swelled and swayed and she searched for the head of David among the throng.

He appeared at her side. She had gone outside for air, sat on a stoop. Under the streetlight he smiled at her. He was very tall. His smile drew her to him, and she felt herself in the presence of something good.

"Hello, stranger," she said. She knew she would remember this day for the rest of her life.

"How're all the patients? Any more falls?" She had told him, before, of patients—men mostly—fainting when blood was drawn, at the sight of the syringe even. She suspected him a faller himself.

"Every day, without fail," she said, smiling. She wanted to dance, but not just yet. He sat down beside her, their arms almost touching.

Minutes passed and nothing happened. She felt him retreat into the depths again. He could not help it. She gazed at his hand resting on his thigh and longed to hold it, make something of it. She sensed a longing in him too. She closed her eyes. She remembered something she had read—that the more desperately a man is in love, the greater the violence he must do his feelings to risk offending the woman he loves by taking her hand.

They began to walk. The night was warm, the streets alive.

She told him again about the place she came from, the family left behind, the father. She wanted desperately to get him back.

"I never knew my father," he said. "My mother reared me and my brother. When I was eight, my cousin told me my father was a bus driver. I'd stare at all the buses going by, at the drivers, wondering . . . Is it you? When I got on a bus, I thought he'd surely know me, he would just *know* me." He threw away his cigarette. "One day when I was walking home from school a bus passed and the driver waved at me, and smiled. I thought it was him—I was certain. For a long time I searched. Now, well, I think . . . he probably wasn't a bus driver at all."

She felt him grow remote once more. She searched her mind for things to say. It was all she could do not to touch him.

"I have to go," he said.

She was stricken. She caught something in his eyes— confusion, anger—as if hijacked by feelings he did not under- stand. She watched him walk away.

"Will you be here next week?" she asked his back, almost whispering. It took all the courage she could muster.

He turned and walked back to her. She felt herself in the lap of the gods. He brought his face to hers and kissed her. She could taste the cigarette.

And then he was gone.

8 Music drifted through open church doors onto the sunny street where she was walking and stopped her in her tracks. She entered the vestibule and read a notice for a lunchtime recital. She listened. First she discerned piano, then cello. She stepped into the dim interior and stood by the baptismal font at the back. A small audience sat in the front pews, the musicians to the side. The notes changed, grew loud and discordant, then softened again and ascended in a pure harmony. Alone, the piano played slow and somber. And then, from the cello, rose the most mournful sound she had ever heard. Beautiful, melancholy, reaching every remote cell. She closed her eyes. With his kiss he had claimed her. He had awoken her soul.

Days passed, each an eternity. She remembered every word, and was by turn exalted, desolate. She had never lived so intensely. At night she sat at her dressing-table mirror. She felt his approach, felt him steal into her, leaving a cold shivery fear at her center, and afterwards a waning numbness. The only cure would be the sight of him. She crawled into bed. In the dark her mouth shaped itself to kiss, re-kiss, grasping at the air in little fish gulps. She bit back the reflex, the trembling mouth. The things that had seemed indecent to think were no longer so: his limbs, his skin, his hand pressed flat on her belly. *Please come back to me.*

She looked out of windows. She drifted, distant and composed, through each working day, the routes and rhythms of trains and subways, streets and corridors, already set into her neural grid. Days off she spent in the library, vaguely dreaming, vaguely sick, or in the park, staring at men walking home from work. In the apartment the fan whirred and she looked out and examined the day.

One evening, alone, at twilight she rose from the table and left her hand on the refrigerator door and felt its faint vibrations. She leaned against it and closed her eyes. The radio was on, low. After what seemed a long time she walked to the window and saw a man on the street below, smoking a cigarette. She thought it was him. She had a vision of herself, dressed in his skin, her arms inside his, her head in his. He raised his face, but it was not him. She remained calm, felt herself possessed of infinite patience. The man threw his cigarette on the pavement and turned and walked away.

She moved from the window. She stood in the middle of the room. So this is love, she thought.

She went down to the drugstore, desperate to be among people. Returning, she was accosted on the street by a bag lady, a face thrust in hers, crazed eyes, wild hair. A mad mouth screaming obscenities at her, shouting out Tess's own thoughts. Shameful thoughts. She froze, trapped under the woman's spell, cursed. Then someone passed and knocked against her and she came to her senses and ran, stumbling, into her building.

The incident shook her to the core. How had that woman known her thoughts—the carnal thoughts that she, Tess, had harbored? This man, this love, had become a disturbance, an interruption in her life. She needed to put an end to it. The following Sunday she visited Molly and Fritz. Oliver was there—she had not seen him in a while. He sat red-eyed, hungover, depressed. Alone for a minute after dinner, she asked good-humoredly about the raven-haired girl. He raised his listless eyes and shrugged.

Molly sat down. "Have you heard from Claire? I wonder if her arm is any better."

"What's wrong with her arm?" Tess asked.

"I don't think it's much . . . She has it ever since Elizabeth was born. It could be arthritis—this family is riddled with arthritis."

She was ashamed. Wrapped in her own selfish fantasies.

That night she called Claire. She could hardly speak.

"How are you, Tess? When are you coming to visit us?" The voice was far away and lonely.

"I'll come soon, I will. In October. I promise. How's your arm?"

"It's much better. It's nothing—just numb from carrying Elizabeth around. But now she's walking."

"And Peter?"

"He's good. He's busy, always busy—the company's expanding. It's all . . . great. They have these family days—I meet the other wives. They're all so pally with each other. We go to parties. Oh, Tess . . . you wouldn't believe what some people get up to." Her voice trailed off.

"Is everything okay, Claire?"

A hesitation. "Yes, of course. Everything's good, Tess . . . Do come out. You promised! I think of you every day."

Anne Beckett's wedding drew near. They had grown close, and Tess longed to pour out her feelings for Anne's cousin, but the dread, and the prospect of shame, if she had misread the signs and imagined it all, prevented her. She contrived to steer conversation towards topics in which his name might arise, but was struck dumb when it did. One night in August, Anne was writing her wedding invitations at the kitchen table, stacking them into a neat pile for posting. Checking names off her list.

"Donal Brennan, my cousin, can't come, but David is definitely coming—he was afraid he mightn't make it. He thinks he'll be shipping out in October."

Her heart took fright. "Has he been drafted?" She had thought the draft applied only to American citizens.

"I don't know. I don't think so. I think he just signed up for the air force. He's being sent to a base in New Jersey in the next few weeks . . ." She thought for a second. "I doubt he'll be flying planes. Maybe paperwork or something."

A while later, after Anne had gone to bed, she found his invitation in the pile and memorized the address.

He was not in the church for the ceremony, or outside on the sunny street where the guests overflowed afterwards. The reception was held in a hotel forty minutes out of the city. When she saw him at the table, seated three places from her in a suit and shirt and tie, and when he looked up and their eyes met, she knew that, for all the times she had remembered him, he had remembered her too. She watched his hands bringing the fork, the glass, to his lips. She saw his wrists and the fine hairs under the cuff of his sleeve and thought of his skin, warm and smooth under the shirt, and she had to look away. She ate little and genteelly, a new refinement arriving of its own accord, as if every limb and organ and nerve was in obeisance, moved to honor the beloved.

"I thought you were a lawyer. Why are you joining the air force?" They were on the terrace. She was flushed from the wine. The light was fading and night lights were coming up on the lawn. She took the cigarette he offered and bent to his lighter's flame.

"I am a lawyer. Anyone can enlist if they're under twenty-five—which I am, just about—so long as they pass the medical."

She frowned. "So you're not being drafted. It's your own choice to go."

He did not answer immediately. She thought of the TV images, helicopters, a burning monk, the words *Saigon*, *Viet Cong*.

"Yes, it's my own choice."

He looked out across the lawn, into the twilight. In the silence that ensued, she arrived at a complete understanding of him. Recalling this moment later, she could not say how she had come to this understanding, only that she had, she had fathomed something deep in him. It was more than fellow feeling. It was as if she had perceived all the joy and fear and pain that had ever entered his heart, and he had let her. For an instant he had let her love him. Her eyes began to fill with tears. It was not with sorrow for his going that she wept, but with a new and gentle longing, a wish that he would get all he had ever wanted. She had an urge to take his tender feeble hand and cover it with her own. She saw him, a small boy again, at the burning tree, standing on a street gazing after buses.

All evening they moved in and out of each other's orbit. She was a little drunk. When the tables were cleared and the band started up, he did not seek her out but waited an hour, until she had grown almost distraught. Finally, she was in his arms, being wafted across the floor. She looked up at his face, inhaled the sweetness of whiskey on his breath. A line from a poem dangled just beyond her consciousness, but she could not pluck down the first word.

"I dreamt about you," he said.

At the bar they could not peel their eyes from each other. Around them, the beat of the music, people dancing. Ice cubes tinkled and sparkled in their glasses. She sipped the amber liquid, felt its heat spread through her. She put a hand on his arm to steady herself and his eyes smiled. They moved to a dim corner, sat on plush red velvet, touching shoulders, arms, thighs. This certain love is melting me, she thought, and leaned into him.

He was carrying her shoes. Her hand was inside his as they climbed stairs. A corridor of crimson carpet, deep, under bare feet, and then the sinking softness of his bed and his face swimming into view. His chest, the glow of uncovered skin. She left a hand on his sternum, his collarbone. She thought of the word *clavicle*, how beautiful it was. Her eyes opened and closed and opened again, and she was gone, drifting, light-headed.

And then, woozy, half dreaming, she gasped at the first hot stab and cried out in pain. She pushed at his chest, tried to pull herself from under him. Frightened, he looked into her eyes, and rolled off. He stroked her cheek tenderly. *Shh, I'm sorry.* A look of sorrow came upon him. She began to crumble. A tear rolled from the corner of her eye. He kissed her eyelids, whispered something she did not hear.

They lay in each other's arms. She did not want to lose him. She pressed herself to him, felt herself yield again. He searched her face, kissed her. He began to move, slowly, gently, his hands caressing her until she felt the swell and ache of her body, the longing to fuse, to be subsumed. She turned her head to the side, repositioned herself under his weight. He seemed to forget himself then, and her. She did not care. She closed her eyes against the pain, both shocking and stirring. She was offering herself to him, and to something larger. She felt herself topple and a point of light, of bright sensation, opened and spread, spacious within her, and pushed her perilously close to a precipice. She had the feeling that he might after all save her, save them both, but then he gasped and shuddered and collapsed on top of her.

She lay there like a stone. She heard footsteps, voices in the corridor. From somewhere far off came the sound of music, as if reaching her through water. She hauled herself from the undertow and staggered to the bathroom and knelt at the toilet bowl. Strands of her hair fell into the vomit. She sat on the floor, trembling, the walls spinning. She ran hot water and sat into the bath, scalding herself.

When she went back to bed he was deeply asleep. She began to shiver. After a time she drifted off. When she woke he was gone, and everything was silent.

9 She tried to make good what was terrible. She tried in her mind to tenderize it, beautify it. More than anything she wanted to cast off shame. She sat in the dark of her apartment and covered her head with her hands. She did not know how to reassemble herself.

She took refuge in the routine of work, in the care of patients and the ordinary talk of her colleagues. For brief interludes she forgot. She arrived on the ward early and left late, speaking and moving with a slowness, a soft remote kindness in every action. An acquiescence, an atonement too, as if relinquishing all claims to the earth. Everywhere, she watched her step, fearful of walking into doors, trees, people. She lowered her head and walked hard and fast on the pavement to beat down words. *Sin. Shame.* In the hall each evening she opened her mailbox with trembling hands, and each evening there came nothing, no word from him. She had thought she had known him. She had known only a small corner of him. Is it possible to know anyone, ever? Taking the stairs in one deliberate step after another, she felt her resistance fade. Hours later, with the TV turned down, fear turned to anger. *Suffer*, her heart cried. *Suffer a little of what I suffer.*

Weeks passed. She was late. She had known from the start— amid the confusion of shame and fear she had expected this too, and now it was almost a relief to be right. To know the worst had come, and the wait was over. In those first nights she had lain awake visualizing the swim: the millions of spawning sperm racing upstream inside her and her mountain of eggs—her twenty-five years' stockpile of ova—waiting to receive them. She said the word aloud, *impregnate*. He has impregnated me. She had the thought that she might be multiply, copiously, pregnant. Her breasts grew tender and swollen and she woke to the taste of metal in her mouth. She sat on the toilet and willed herself to expel it. Nauseated, she leaned over the edge of the sink. She ran the bath and sat in boiling-hot water. In her mind's eye she saw diagrams from her biology books, altered and nightmarish now—blown-up uteruses housing grotesque bodies with large heads and bulging eyes and torsos enfolded in dark creaturely skin.

At the mouth of sleep she tried to reach him, to dream him back. She could bear anything if he appeared. She listened to the ticking of her brain, hyperalert to the minute register of cells dividing and multiplying in the new body, the new brain, inside her. Then dawn arrived and with it the calamity of a new day.

Night after night, she contemplated her options. She ventured down avenues that frightened and sickened her. Words, unspeakable words, remembered from books and magazine articles and hearsay. She stared at the ceiling. It need not be terrible. There were people who could assist, direct her—the word was *procure*—if she had the courage to ask. But never in her whole life had she had one iota of courage. She had sought, always, silent consent for everything she had done—as if she were without volition, as if a father or mother or God himself sat permanently on her right shoulder, holding sway over her thoughts and actions. And when consent was not gleaned, or was felt to be withheld, she resumed her position of quiet passivity. It was not this alone she suffered from now, but terror, and a complete paralysis of the soul.

She lay awake, dried-out salt deposits on her cheeks. She had prolonged hope to almost unendurable limits. He was gone. All glory, all happiness, had gone with him, and she was left imperiled. The memory of the night flooded back, their bodies. She had seen him in his private throes, at his most secret, defenseless self. Did that not count for something? She wore herself out thinking, her lips bitten and bruised. Finally, she slept. She dreamt she was in a big old house, fleeing from someone along dark corridors. She ran to the farthest room and locked the door, her heart a sea of panic. She heard footsteps, saw the handle turn. She ran to a window, saw that the glass was veined with cracks, millions of cracks, barely holding, and the walls the same, and the ceiling—everything about to shatter. If she as much as left a finger on anything, or stirred, or breathed, a ton of glass would cascade down on top of her.

She felt someone in the room when she woke. She closed her eyes again. Madness, she thought. Yet she felt something, a foreboding. A memory returned, of being alone in the chapel one evening as a child, and in the haunting sacred silence being seized by a fear that the Blessed Virgin would appear and speak to her, claim her.

The room had an eerie glow now, a strange transient beauty. She sat up. The glow intensified, and she felt its dangerous intoxicating allure. She stepped onto the cold linoleum and crossed the floor and raised the window blind and there, in the building across, a fire blazed. Flames rose out of windows and leapt upwards, licking at the bricks. She felt its heat, its burning brightness on her face. Panicked, she ran to the door, ran back again. She tried to see into the heart of the fire, beyond it. She imagined rooms, furniture like her own, paint blistering, ceilings buckling and collapsing. Everything consumed. She saw her own reflection in the glass. The whine of sirens carried from the far side of the building. She shrank back from the window into the ghostly glow of the room, the fire's haunting crackle in her ears.

She saw it as an omen. Who would save her? Who in the world would save her? Who would remember her? She was already burning. A fallen woman.

Over the city, dawn was breaking. She was on the roof, the light diffuse. A cluster of flowerpots sat in the corner, the flowers wilting, their best days over. She leaned over the wall. Far below the first of the day's cars glided by. To her left she saw the tree-tops in the park. Soon they would shed their leaves. Easterfield's leaves were probably gone, blown away now. More than a year had passed since she'd seen those trees, the beeches, the injured ash. Time, moment by moment, trickling away to bring her to now. She kept her eyes on the trees, the rays of the rising sun just then touching the uppermost branches. She could not go back. She could not face her father. He had raised four motherless daughters, delivered them into womanhood without blemish, and he had not been found wanting—his moral compass had sufficed. She remembered his face. She could hear him. *Street walker . . . Bringing disgrace down on top of me . . . Driving me into an early grave . . . Your mother . . . Your mother . . . Don't ever darken this door again . . .*

> *My dearest Tess,*
> *How are you? I keep hoping you'll come. I had a letter from Maeve last week. Poor Dadda. I remember what Mamma said to Evelyn and me before she died: Ye have a good father but ye have a hard father. When I think of him now, sick, I'm filled with pity. I didn't always see it this way, but now my heart is crying for him, and all his struggles.*

And the way he always stayed loyal to her. So much harder for a man.

I long to see you, Tess. When will you come? Write anyway, tell me how you are. I dreamt of you the other night, that you were a little girl again and you fell into the old well. Oh, aren't dreams terrible things?

I hope you're living it up there in the city. I imagine you on summer evenings walking downtown with a handsome man. Oliver too, with that girl you told me about. All of you together.

And you with your beautiful soul shining out of you. Oh Tess, you're worth ten of the rest of us.

God bless,
Claire

One day she saw that the trees were bare. It was November; the seasons had changed unknown to her. On the ward she placed pills in an old woman's hand, the skin parchment thin. The woman was watching TV, almost in a trance. *As the World Turns.* Her hand brought the pills to her lips, then halted and hovered there. Tess touched the hand and guided it to its destination. A moment later, stretching up to replace an IV bag, she felt constrained, her uniform tight, her body constricted. She glanced down and saw the swell of her breasts, fuller than before, and her heart dropped. Soon, her belly would begin to bulge. A hush fell on the ward and when she looked up all eyes were trained on the TV. The program had been interrupted for a news bulletin. The newscaster, uncertain, moved his head from script to camera and back again. The president had been shot. People let out little gasps. Tess stood before the TV. She remained there, staring, when the commercial break came. Niagara laundry starch, nuSoft fabric softener. Chewing gum for heartburn.

Two days later, at home, she watched the killer being killed live on TV. And later, over and over, the president's motorcade speeding along the Dallas streets, his beautiful wife crawling, scrambling in her blood-splattered suit, frantic to get out of the car. Tess watched, stunned. Why was Jackie abandoning him in his hour of need? Did she not want to hold him, die with him, even? Or does self-preservation trump love? She turned from the TV. Then the truth hit her—Jackie was climbing to get to her children. Her frantic scramble was to get to them, wherever they were, fling herself over them, save them.

The next day a somber silence fell again on the ward and all eyes were glued to the TV. Outside the cathedral, the president's small son stepped forward and saluted his father's casket. Around Tess, everyone wept. She feared the end of the world again. Everything would be extinguished, the child inside her too. She was jolted by the gun salute at the grave. *Bang. Bang. Bang.* She felt the impact and put a hand to her stomach.

That night, she watched it all, over and over. The funeral procession, the marching cadets, the prayers and intonations. *There is an appointed time for everything . . . a time to be born and a time to die . . .* She rose and went into the kitchen. She lifted a small jug of milk from the table and carried it to the sink. She thought of Mike Connolly rising from his stool after milking a cow, then pouring warm milk from the bucket into a saucer for the cat. Once he'd put her kittens into a sack and drowned them in a barrel of water. She looked out at the night. She began to pour the milk down the sink. She paused and poured it over her hands, first one, then the other. Then she ran her milky palms down her face.

"What have you done, Tess? Jesus, what have you done? *How did this happen?*"

She was standing in Aunt Molly's living room, her hand

holding the edges of her herringbone tweed coat together against the bulge of her stomach. She looked at the floor. In the next room Fritz coughed.

"I'll get the blame, you know. I'm supposed to be looking after you. Your father will blame me. *Jesus, Mary and Joseph*, Tess, what did you do? Who's the father? You'd better be getting married, madam."

She vowed never again to explain herself. She did not see Oliver—he had not been in touch for months. One day she bought a thin gold wedding band and at work smiled weakly and nodded, yes, yes, she'd gotten married. Outside of work she saw few people. Anne Beckett had moved down to the main campus of the hospital soon after her marriage and, having no wish to take in a stranger, Tess kept on the apartment alone, a decision that caused financial strain for some time. She let the friendship with Anne wane, wanting no reminder of the child's paternity. She resolved never to reveal it. She resolved to erase him from her memory, think him and reason him out of her life. She placed herself in the care of an obstetrician, a small, round middle-aged man with tiny eyes and a kind demeanor who made Tess feel so safe that, after each consultation, she wished he was the father. Evenings, boarding a bus or a subway train, her eyes involuntarily scanned the aisles for young, earnest-looking men, and, finding one, she sat next to him with a familiar ease, her wedding finger on view, as if she were his, and he hers and the swollen belly theirs, and devised for that short ride an alternative life.

My darling Tess,

What you must be going through. Oh, how I wish I could be with you. I am there, in heart and mind, you know. If you would only call me, or answer the phone. There is nothing to fear, Tess. Please talk to me. I will not judge you. I will ask

*no questions—I want no answers, except to know that you
are safe, that you will be all right. And you __will__, Tess. It will
all come right in the end. Are you taking care of yourself? Are
you seeing a doctor? Please, please, let me know how you are.
And do not despair.*

*I would come, Tess—I would fly there in the morning—if
I could, but the children. And this problem of mine. I cannot
hold a cup of tea now without spilling it, and my legs are like
lead so that I stagger all the time—it looks like I have drink
taken. Even my writing has gone shaky. They've done tests,
but nothing is confirmed yet.*

*Say a prayer for me, Tess, and I pray for you. And for
Oliver, wherever he is. We are all orphans again.*

> *With all my love, always,*
> *Claire*

Snow fell in December. Alone, she wept. She wrote and rewrote
and tore up each letter to Claire. Everywhere on the streets carol
singers, lights, scenes of joy. She worked on Christmas Eve,
spent Christmas Day alone, shunning Molly and Fritz, declin-
ing an invitation from Anne Beckett. She went to eleven o'clock
Mass and in the afternoon cooked her dinner and propped a
book on the table, reading as she ate. Later, she watched *The
Andy Williams Christmas Show*, interrupted by ads with families
around dinner tables, rosy-cheeked children around fires. She
permitted herself a brief vision of the future, and a quiet hope
whispered itself to her. In the evening, in the lamp-lit bedroom,
she stood before the mirror and lifted her dress, and stroked the
gleaming globe of her belly. She felt vast, large with life, and
she was moved by her own fecundity. *He* had put this into her,
he had filled her up. She was the carrier of his flesh and blood,
his skin and bone, their co-joined cells dividing and multiplying,

and the new thing ripening within her. She gazed in the mirror. She was no longer blemished, but beautiful. She wished she could remain in this gestational state forever, live her whole life in this perfect state of waiting.

At twilight she went out and walked the streets to Inwood Hill Park, marveling at the light fall of snow, glistening, pristine in the streetlights. In the distance, the city murmured. Above, a blue-black sky. She longed to know where on this earth he was tonight, on what continent, under what sky. She walked along the park's perimeter, ice glittering on bare branches overhead. She felt the child stir. She walked for a long time, looking up at lighted apartments, frosted trees, the moon. The night was unbearably beautiful. How had she traversed the earth to arrive here, at this splendor?

Dear David,
  I would like to talk to you. Perhaps you could call me.
                                        Yours kindly,
                                        Tess Lohan

She wrote it twice, on identical greeting cards, her address and phone number on the left-hand side. She posted one to the address she had memorized, the other to McGuire Air Force Base in New Jersey. Her hand hovered at the mouth of the mailbox and a second later the tiny sound of the letters dropping left a heartbreaking echo inside her.

One evening in late February, after an eight-hour shift and a subway suicide that disrupted the A train, she trudged home along the streets in the rain. Inside, she paused on the third-floor landing to get her breath, her feet, her back, aching. A door opened and a small neat black woman, whom Tess had often seen on the stairs, stepped out and placed trash in the refuse chute, and then turned. Tess went to take a step, but faltered. Their eyes met and the woman approached.

"Honey, are you okay? You don't look so good." Eyes shining out of a dark face, black hair, wide like a halo around her head. She took a step closer. "I know you, don't I? You're the Irish girl from upstairs. You feel like a drink of water, honey?" She put a hand on Tess's arm. Suddenly tears came. Wordlessly, the woman led her through the open door to a lighted room, to small children eating and playing in corners, warm. Eyes shining like their mother's. A glorious place, the hum of Heaven. The woman was named Willa. Tess sat at the table and thought she was dreaming. She could not speak. A bamboo cage hung from the ceiling and inside, on a perch, sat a dark bird with a collar of yellow feathers. Willa was watching her watching the bird. "It's a mynah bird," she said.

Under the table Tess slipped off her shoes and placed her feet on the cool floor. She drank a glass of chilled pear juice. She ate salty crackers spread with cheese. The bird gazed down at her with a benign eye. Then it opened its beak. "Talk to me," it said.

10

The pain struck at dawn. Willa came. In the hospital foyer her waters broke. She looked down at her drenched shoes and began to cry.

That evening when it was all over she thought she had scaled Everest, stood at its peak, exhilarated. The next morning the enormity of it all hit her. She had brought forth life, rendered human something from almost nothing, and this power, this ability to create, overwhelmed her.

She did not take to the child. The light down on his skin resembled fur. She could not bear to touch the head, the unknitted bones of his crown. She thought of him as half-hatched, not quite finished. She was not in her right mind. Her body had been riven open, pummeled, her innards displaced. A disgust at her physical self took hold, at the engorged breasts, the bleeding. I am a cow, she thought. But cows are good mothers. On the ward fathers came, brought flowers, cradled infants. She closed her curtain. They brought her the child. Alone, he frightened her, and she rang the bell for them to come and take him away.

On the third day she rose and showered. At feeding time she stood outside the nursery and looked in. He was the only one left. She felt his profound loneliness. Not long born he might drift away again into cold interstellar spaces. She walked to the nurses' station, her heart pounding. She put down his bottle and stared at the face behind the desk. "I want to give my baby up for adoption," she said.

All day long she lay thinking, sleeping, crying. She pictured him in other arms, new voices and scents washing over him, colliding inside him. She imagined his confusion, his striving to discern each voice, to retrieve hers in the chaos, until finally, gathering in his cries, he grew mute and surrendered.

She tried to sleep. She dreamt she was back in Easterfield, roaming the dark rooms upstairs. At the end of the hall she found a toddler hunkered down in a corner. He had been there a long time, surviving on nothing. He had something in his hand that he raised to his mouth and bit. She peered closer and saw it was a human finger—hers, her index finger.

When she woke, night had fallen and the ward was in semi-darkness, the other mothers all sleeping. She got out of bed and walked to the nursery. She feared it was too late, like a lamb too long parted from its mother to take. At the sight of him through the glass her arms ached for his weight and she rushed to him. Trembling, she bundled him up in his blanket and fled on weak legs along the corridor, down two flights of stairs. At the front entrance the night guard stepped into her path and, smiling, laid a gentle hand on the bundle. "It's a nice night out there, ma'am, but still, maybe you'd like to get a sweater?" She looked out at the street. She looked into the man's eyes, down at the sleeping child, then back at the man's face. Confused, bewildered, she let him lead her by the arm to the elevator and back up to the ward.

The next morning, with the child asleep beside her, she picked up a pen and wrote: *You have a son. His name is Theo.*

Nothing was more fully or finely felt, ever again, as the days and nights of that first summer with the child. Her eyes were permanently trained on his and his were locked on hers, a flow of wondrous love streaming between them. *Flesh of my flesh, blood of my blood.* She took him into her bed at night, wanted to put him back inside her. In the morning she shaded his face from the sun slanting through the blinds. She put soft seamless clothes on him, so that no harshness would touch his skin. She did not ever want to leave the apartment or break the spell. She wanted no interruption, no sight or sound or dissonance from the world to dull his radiance or endanger him.

Little by little, the sense of impending doom that had stalked her for so long began to recede. She wrote to Claire, told her everything. Each day Willa came, sometimes with a child or two in tow, once bringing her husband, Darius, to build a stand for the Moses basket. Willa took the child from Tess and, with remarkable ease, carried him in the crook of her arm as she cooked and tidied and talked. She introduced Tess to other mothers in the building. One day she brought her own pram onto the landing and together they carried it downstairs and the two women walked their children in the sun. On a park bench, in the shade of trees, Willa told Tess her life story. Born in Mississippi, she never knew her daddy. Her mother moved north to Detroit when Willa and her sister were small. At seventeen she met Darius and knew instantly he was a good man. They married and moved to New York, where he got a job driving the A train. For extra income she minded kids—the Gallaghers on the second floor, the O'Dowds on the fourth—while their mothers went out to work.

In October she left Theo with Willa and returned to work at the hospital. Each evening she rushed home, exhausted, sleep-deprived, and swept him up in her arms, like a woman in love. One evening when she entered her apartment a telegram lay on the floor. *Father died peacefully last night. Tell Oliver. Denis.* Shaken, she put Theo into the pram and took the subway down to 181st Street, imagining, as the train rushed through the tunnel, that she heard the bawling of newly weaned lambs beyond the walls. She rang Molly's doorbell and waited, nervous, headstrong, but no longer ashamed. The two women embraced, and Fritz lifted out the child. They called Claire. Tess could scarcely make out what Claire was saying. She had Lou Gehrig's disease. Tess cried into the phone, and together they grieved their father.

The child's hair grew fair, his eyes blue. Early one spring morning when she came off night duty she collected Theo at Willa's and wheeled him, still sleeping, to the park, and sat on a bench. She loved this hour, with almost no one around, and the hush of the night and the sleeping patients still lingering in her. She grew open and alert to the newness of the morning, the possibilities of the day. She looked at the new green leaves—so many shades of green—and almost had to shield her eyes from their brightness, their newborn beauty. Too much beauty, she thought. And too much happiness, these days. Too much happiness frightened her. She pulled back from these thoughts and looked around. An old man was approaching along the path, as if making for her. She began to gather up her things, but then he was there, standing before her. He asked the child's name. Theo, she replied, warily.

"Theodore," he said. "I had a son by that name. We lost him to glandular fever. It was during the Depression. We were living in Tent City." He sat next to her and told her the whole story. Theo was sitting up in the pram, his eyes fixed on the old man, and she saw for the first time what he might look like—the boy emerging out of the baby—and the mannerisms he might have, in the years ahead. She had the sudden urge to confide in this stranger, befriend him, make him a surrogate grandfather. A gift for him too.

The old man looked at Tess with rheumy eyes. "He was our

only child. My wife died twenty-three years ago." She saw his clean-shaven face, his neat clothes. She got a glimpse of his life, his daily routine, the order and discipline, rising and cooking and walking. He turned his gaze back to the child and she felt him wander. She wanted to say something, call him back from his sorrow.

"This is my love child," she said.

He nodded abstractly and his eyes drifted off along the path in the wake of other strollers. Then he got up, walked over to the stone tables where old men played chess on summer evenings. She watched him sit, alone, and stare at the checkered tabletop.

That night in her kitchen, she said it again, *love child*. Born against the odds, more hard-won, more precious, than all others. She had not elected to be a mother. In the next room the child whimpered. She listened, waited for him to return to sleep. She would have liked to have the father there beside her, for him to hear that whimper too. The memory of his face returned. The memory of his beauty hurt her mind. On the radio Billie Holiday began to sing. *More than you know.* She thought of the city beyond the apartment, lights twinkling in high-rise buildings all around her. Inside, nests of families. He could not give what he had not got. She began to weep. She knew that a great part of love was mercy. What she wished for then, what she wanted more than anything else, was for all ultimate good to come to him.

On Good Friday, in the ward, she received a call from the front desk telling her she had visitors downstairs. Molly and Fritz were waiting in chairs, and when she saw them her heart lurched. Molly rose, came towards her, her face crumbling. "She's gone, Tess. Claire is gone."

That afternoon, she accompanied two elderly patients to the hospital chapel for the gospel readings of the Passion. A choir and a small orchestra performed Bach. Once, as a child, she had fainted in the packed church during the long Good Friday readings. Claire, or Evelyn perhaps, had carried her outside, her bottom lip bleeding from the fall, and put her down on the grass. She remembered coming to, the sun, the light. She had felt resurrected. Now she stood for the long reading. Peter denies Christ three times, the cock crows. The musicians played the opening chorus, and it took hold of her and she was brought down by the terror, the torment, the fury. Peter's anguish. *Herr, Herr, Herr.* She sat, stricken. The priest began again, and she was there by the cross with the men, the weeping women. She felt the crown of thorns, the sword piercing his side. She closed her eyes to the serene music, the sorrow in the soloist's voice, the last still note. She became bereft. She was with Christ on Calvary, with Claire in Gethsemane. *"It is finished," he said. And he bowed his head and gave up his spirit.*

That night she went up on the roof and lit a cigarette. The sounds of the city rose and fused into one deep hum in her ears. She inhaled deeply and the nicotine spiked her lungs. Lighted windows surrounded her, eyes watching her in the dark. She stood in the center and turned, dizzy from the nicotine. Above her, an unbounded sky, infinite, too much to behold. Her grief was as large as the sky. How had it come to this? She lay down on the roof and curled up and Claire's face came to mind. All her faculties, her senses, were quiet now. In a few days she would be laid to rest, side by side with strangers, under a California sun. What these months must have cost her. The small girl, the boy, presented to her one last time, unable to raise a hand to touch their heads, groping for words through wasted muscles and withered vocal cords. The sound of their play later in the day drifting up from the backyard, while indifferent angels sat and stared as she faded out in a darkened room, fighting off Heaven until Heaven won, and she vanished.

She heard a thud. She raised her head, scanned the rooftop. She was alone. She peered into the corner and saw the door, closed. She jumped up, ran, saw that the plank of wood used to prop it open had been kicked away. The janitor had come, locked up for the night. She flung herself at the steel door, pounded her fists, called out his name. Blind with panic, she picked up the plank and lashed it against the metal, then paused, listened out for a voice or footsteps inside. She ran across the rooftop to the west wall, the east wall, the north and south, back and forth until the space in between increased with each crossing. She leaned over, called down eight stories to the street below. She searched other rooftops, windows, for faces, the image of Theo in his crib three floors below tormenting her. Over and back she ran, calling out until her voice grew hoarse and tears came. She slid down against the wall, pulled her cardigan tight around her, and began to pray.

Above her the sky was a vault. Stars looked down on the whole round earth. She felt herself remote. She was staring into emptiness. In the dark and deepening shades she divined a cry. She felt the child stir and his eyelids flicker, and every breath, every minute sound, reached her distinctly. She held her own breath and his cry came again from within her, loud and soft, hypnotizing her, twisting, circling, echoing from ear to ear inside her head. *Shh, go back to sleep.* His eyes opening, registering the room, the light shining in from the hall. His small arms starting to free themselves, raising a thumb to his mouth. For a while he lay still, alert for any sound, then rose from under the covers, held on to the bars of the crib. *Shh, shh*, she whispered. She strained to reach him. He started to whimper, then paused, listened. She was not coming. He began to sob. The sob became a cry, and the cry a howl. His howls pierced her. She summoned every power and willed him near her.

Exhausted, he threw himself down on the covers, his cheeks

flushed and tear-stained, his little fists yielding. *Shh, rock-a-bye baby*. She hummed, whispered, strove until there existed a perfect consonance between his breath and hers, his heart and hers. Hours passed. The chill of the night entered her bones.

She stirred. Cold and stiff, she tried to rise. The whole building listed, tilted in the night, and she swayed and slid back down. She drew up her knees. She wished she were made of stone. She peered at a narrow gap, black, between the roof boards, and her mind slipped in, bored a hole down into the dark, a channel through the heart of the building to where the child lay. She poured herself in. Falling, falling. Walls pressing against her. Coffin walls, quarry walls. Orchard walls. Well walls.

All night long she drifted in and out of dreams, visions, prayers. At dawn the sun broke over the rooftops, and the city stirred. She heard the clang of metal and the steel door fell open. To the west a plane rose slowly, climbed into the sky.

11 The child's existence turned a plain world to riches. Her life raised up like this, the child giving point and purpose to each day, the care of him transforming her, widening and deepening her.

Something else, too, accrued. Everywhere her heart softened towards mankind. The minor irritations—the slow strollers on the pavement at rush hour, a broken elevator, a long line in a café—were shed. A tenderness entered her actions, a softness in her tone of voice. She found unbearable a raised voice, a blaring horn, a rough hand on a patient. She saw vulnerability everywhere—old women in shopping aisles, the bums and drunks and hoboes on the subway, the blind, the lame, the stray dogs—the voiceless and defenseless on every corner. One day she stopped before a broken branch on the pavement, and when she looked up, the bare wound on the bough grieved her.

A small circle of people attached to her life—Willa, Molly and Fritz, a few colleagues, and at a further remove, the Irish families in her building. She saw Anne Beckett only once, before Anne and her husband returned to Ireland. Neither of them mentioned the child—there was no need, they were unlikely to meet again. Tess wrote to Claire's husband in California and offered to have the children visit. His reply, when it came, was polite but noncommittal, and between the lines Tess found the hint of a new love. She thought of the boy and girl in the years to come, imagining their lives, in a house with a new mother, on a beach with a new brother.

It was with Willa that she was most herself. With Willa she found an affinity that she did not find with her colleagues or with the other mothers in her building. It had existed from the start, this understanding. She saw how Willa treated people, her ease with children—how she mollified them—and from her example Tess learned how to be a mother. She noted the patience and grace with which Willa conducted herself when subjected to racial barbs and insults, sometimes inflicted by Tess's own compatriots. She was in thrall to Willa's life too, to her appetite for life, her freedom, the order she brought. Her apartment was warm, noisy, full of cooking smells and chatter and arguments, and Willa at the heart of it. Tess tried to emulate her ways but an air of quietude seemed to hang in her own rooms always, as if something vital was missing.

Theo grew strong and healthy. He was almost too beautiful. With this thought came a vague feeling of premonition, a presentiment. When he was two and a half Willa stood him against her kitchen wall one day and measured him. "Two foot one," she announced. "He'll be triple that, you know—six foot three when he's fully grown." She winked. "Tall daddy, huh, Tess?"

The next day she wrote three letters to Ireland, warm, factual, unapologetic, and enclosed a photograph of Theo in each. She did not mention his paternity. She received no reply from Denis, and those from Evelyn and Maeve, while expressing mild congratulations in the final lines, were brief and wary and distant. They stopped short of condemnation, and Tess knew that this was merely because her morally compromised life was sufficiently removed from theirs so as not to incur shame. Her heart sank reading the letters, but as the days passed and she remembered the country she had left behind, and placed herself in her sisters' shoes, she understood, and forgave. On the subway one evening she contemplated an alternative life back there. A pall grew, a feeling of ennui, at the thought of the daily mundane, the restraint, the stasis. The feeling of things closing off, closing down. She could never have kept Theo. It seemed to her now to be a place without dreams, or where dreaming was prohibited. Here, life could be lived at a higher, truer pitch. Though her own was a timid life, there was, since Theo's birth, a yearning towards motion and spirit and vitality. As she walked along the Manhattan streets, she felt a sudden elation. She started to see possibilities everywhere, and it was this feeling of possibility—even if she did not always avail herself of it—this vibrancy and passion that were essential to life. Perhaps that was the very source of her anxiety, she thought, the mark of all anxiety: the acute awareness of the endless possibilities that can simultaneously imperil and enhance us, and all that might be lost or gained. And the terrible tension that exists when everything hangs on a moment, that moment when one may take a leap of faith, or not. It is choice, then, she thought, freedom of choice, that is the cause of all anxiety.

When she was on night duty Theo slept at Willa's and, in turn, Tess had Willa's two boys sleep over occasionally, a small black face waking up on either side of Theo, like brothers. Theo went to the playground with them, played on the landing, ran up and down the stairs with them and the Gallagher and O'Dowd kids. And yet a deep solitariness attached to him. She watched the way his eyes followed a moving ball, a Frisbee, a dog running up to him in the park. She saw him pause between thought and action, faltering on the brink of speech, his face solemn. She watched him endlessly, alert to the moment when he became aware of his own separateness. At those times it seemed to her that he had been inevitable. He had always been deemed. The surprise was that it was to her he was born. *Succubus. Incubus.*

On dark winter mornings he came into her room and lay sleepily across her body, their heartbeats intersecting across skin and bone and cloth. She rose and dressed in the dark and made breakfast before waking him. They sat at the kitchen table as the sky lightened or snow fell soundlessly, eerily, outside, and he sat, rapt, reflected in its strange white light.

She told him about Easterfield. She led him through the rooms. She saw again every table, every chair and bed and sideboard, just as it had been. A pink eiderdown on a bed. A gray coat on the back of Mike Connolly's door. The view out over fields through a pane of old wavy glass. The scent of apples, chicken meal soaking in the back kitchen, her father calling for his tea. She had no photographs for him. One morning she drew a picture: the avenue, the trees, the gravel courtyard. Her hand hovered over the page, not knowing how to come at the house. So she drew the laurel tree. Later, in Willa's apartment, he added a house, birds, Captain. She had a vision of him there, running down the stairs with Evelyn's and Maeve's kids, rushing to strike the gong in the front hall, then opening the door, tumbling onto the gravel and racing towards the orchard, or out into the fields.

One morning at work she stood with the medical team at the bedside of an elderly man. She was struck by a sense of something familiar in the old man's face. When the doctors moved along to the next patient she moved too, and then, feeling something, glanced back. He was staring at her. All morning long she was troubled. In the afternoon she went to take his blood pressure.

"How is the boy?" he asked.

Her heart jumped. "He's well, thank you." She could not look at him.

She rolled up his pajama sleeve. As she pumped the cuff, their eyes met.

"Does Theodore see his father? Every boy needs a father."

She did not reply. As she walked away, rage at his audacity flared in her.

The next morning he was mute. His name was Boris. He did not register her presence. She took his pulse, his blood pressure, measured his urine output. After breakfast, with the help of a nursing assistant, she washed him. She sponged the wasted muscles of his arms, his thighs, his buttocks. He was silent and compliant, almost meek. She lifted each hand, turned it over, saw the veins, blue, through the skin. She remembered his story on the park bench. She brought the sponge to his chest, over the sparse white hairs, the rib cage. She was aware of his heart, beating rapidly, like a trapped sparrow. She washed him all over, and dried him gently with a towel. The clock on the wall struck twelve. She fixed his bed, puffed up his pillows. She felt a great calm, a composure, in every act. Then she stood still. Down the corridor the lunch carts rattled. A nurse went by, pushing a patient in a wheelchair. She looked around the ward—at the chair by the wall, the sink in the corner, the man in the bed, people passing in the corridor. It is this, all of these things, she thought, that confer reality. All at once she felt grounded, compatible with the world and the presence of things in it.

When her shift ended she approached the old man's bed. He had no one. After a long time he opened his eyes.

"You're back," he said.

"I am." She was sitting on a chair.

He smiled faintly. She felt the weight of recent years, the crushing loneliness, bearing down on her. He would have been a good father, this old man. A scene appeared before her, and all that might have been possible seemed at hand.

"Is there anyone—a friend—you'd like me to call?" she asked.

He shook his head. He was very old. "They're all gone." He turned towards her. "I used to play chess with them," he said.

"I was good! When I was young—in my twenties—I almost made grand master." His face brightened.

"I never learned to play," she said. A little flow of urine trickled into his bag.

"I fell in love with it when I was a kid—I fell in love with the chessmen first, the bishop, the knight. Every game is an odyssey, you know." He cleared his throat. "I played all over, in California, everywhere. Once, at an Olympiad, I competed against an African boy. He was about thirteen—he didn't know his birthday. He never spoke. He had malaria when he was ten and died for two days, but then came back. He spent every day of his life back home foraging for food.

"I played a man in the Ukraine for years. Igor. We mailed our moves to each other. We never met. A game could take a whole year." He smiled. "Patience is a great thing."

She wondered how it would feel to have one great passion.

"Where are you from?" she asked.

"Russia. The Black Sea, a town called Anapa. I have no memory of it. I came here when I was a boy. I remember coming over on the ship, huddled up with my brother."

After a while he asked, "Do you believe in God?" He was thinking of the African boy who had died and come back, or his dead son. Or himself, maybe.

"Yes," she said. "And you?"

He considered for a few moments. He spoke slowly, softly. "In chess you feel it, you know . . . something. It's involuntary—my hand reached out of its own accord all those years to make those moves."

His eyes drifted to the window. They were high up. The sun had gone down. The city lay all around them. After a while he spoke again.

"There is, in some of us, an essential loneliness . . . It is in you."

She looked away. They were quiet for a long time. "You know

95

something?" he said then. He was staring at a spot at the end of the bed. "I could fit my whole life on one page. I could write it all down on a single page." He turned and looked into her eyes. "And I am astonished that it is over and I am here, at the end."

A few nights later, when she came on duty, she found him in a room assigned to the dying, no longer conscious. Near midnight, with the lights low and the other patients sleeping, she sat with him. She had a need to talk to him, the living to the almost dead. His long body lay beneath the bedclothes, his breath shallow. She touched his hand. He had left a clarity, an intense burn, on her. She leaned close, stroked his head, the wisps of white hair. She left her hand on his forehead. There would be no one to wash him or wake him. She felt the tip of his nose, his fingers, icy cold. She sat back and waited. "Not long now," she whispered.

The following night she sat at the kitchen table cutting grocery coupons from the newspaper. Theo was asleep in his room and the radio was on, low. Now and then the steam pipes hissed, then sighed. She hummed along to the song on the radio. *I would rather go blind, boy, than to see you walk away.* She thought of a life fitting on one page. She had always had a need to live by inner signs and had been in perpetual waiting for them to break through. In their absence she had gone blindly on, abiding, making few human measurings.

And yet now in this time, in this life with Theo, there was calm. She felt it a vocation. And she was, she thought, the kind who needed a vocation, to be given over to one thing. She smiled. In another life she might have been a nun. A bride of Christ, her whole being turned over to prayer and reflection, a dissolution of her corporeal self. On the radio a saxophone played. She tilted her head, each plaintive note reaching her. She was a mother, a nurse. These were good things, sure and pure and constant. She need not be afraid. There were worse things. She thought of David. His face floated before her, and with it the germ of an ache. Would there ever come another night, another time, another man, to match that brief all-consuming union? The scene of their lovemaking surfaced. The dreamy feeling, the intoxicating evening, the desire that went awry.

Suddenly the lightbulb flickered and the radio crackled. She heard the rumble of thunder nearby and a flash of lightning lit the building opposite. The bulb flickered again, and went out. She sat still, in the darkness, waiting for the next eruption. If only there had been a second time with him, a second chance to make good that night, to make right that wrong. She had been too happy. Such happiness carried danger at its heart, the seed of its own demise.

When the child was five he started at the Good Shepherd School. Willa took him by the hand and led him and her own kids and the Gallaghers—a trail of small children—along the streets to the school door. On her mornings off Tess herself took him and he strode ahead of her, advancing like he already knew his way, fair and strong and beautiful. After school on summer days he poked in the borders in the park and pressed his face into the grass. She was reminded of Captain nosing in the undergrowth at Easterfield, privy to scents and sounds and hidden wonders—a myriad of minuscule things. She thought that the child sensed this too—the teemingness, the intoxication, the mystery of the physical world.

He learned to read quickly, drawn deep and enchanted by stories. She told him folktales from her own school days, the Salmon of Knowledge, the Children of Lir. She took him to the library, to Mass on Sundays. She wanted him to know all she held dear, everything that would make rapturous his heart. Heedless of his surroundings, he was drawn to solitary activities, fascinated by singular things. He had a hunger to know everything, and year after year his enthrallment grew: birds, trees, the stars and planets, the moon landing, the human body—the boundless universe—all subject to his penetrating intensity. Sometimes, overexcited and overwhelmed by the approach of some dizzying new project, he paled and vomited. He was stepping outside the range of normal awareness into another domain. She sensed inner rhapsodies, an antique state of mind, felicities he could scarcely bear. Occasionally, among other kids, she observed a hesitancy in him, a caution that troubled her. Hyperalert, eager to join in, but guarded, conflicted, wary that what he felt inside—the raptures and ecstasies—might be visible, and mark him out for ridicule or shunning.

"What's your book about?" she asked one evening when he was eight. She stood behind him, smoothed his hair. A time would come when she would not be able to touch him thus.

"Ants. An ant city," he said, engrossed. He did not look up.

When she went to turn out his light, the ant book lay across his chest, and she imagined him drifting to sleep a while before, the ants pulsing in his brain. She took the book into the kitchen. She had not known such subterranean marvels existed. Minute creatures who were master builders. She gazed at the drawings of tiny insects bearing gigantic loads on their backs, pushing mountains of matter with their heads, their delicate antennae foretelling obstacles up ahead. In the dark of deserts there were networks of tunnels in the sand, terraces, towers, refuse heaps. She was filled with awe at the complex social order they created, the castes of workers, the division of labor, the labyrinthine city. *God's architects*. Guided, impelled, by what? Instinct? Divine intervention? She lingered over a drawing of an ant, the compound eyes, the mandibles, the thorax and abdomen, the wings shed after flight. She was mesmerized. Here in her kitchen that evening, oblivious to everything, the child had been transported, lost in the ant city, tumbling into tunnels, into ants' lives. Seeing with their ant eyes and beholding their city, their Jerusalem. Their Jerusalem becoming his Jerusalem.

When he was nine or ten she took him out to Brooklyn one Saturday, to a birthday party at the home of Priscilla, an Italian-American girl who nursed with her. Priscilla and her husband and son lived on a quiet street with neat lawns and cars in driveways. Tess stood in the hall and Theo moved away to join the others. She saw through to the backyard and the adults and children moving about. In the evening when she returned, he did not want to leave. Something in that house, in that family, had favored itself to him. "Let him stay, Tess," Priscilla said. "We'll drop him back tomorrow."

She walked along the street. It was February. She looked in windows, at living rooms with TVs, lamps, open fires. The lives of others. She had not felt this way before: *less*, in his eyes. She understood what he had seen, what he had been denied, and she was bereft. His life was wanting. She had not ever baked him a birthday cake or put up balloons—his birthdays had been celebrated in Willa's apartment after school. She had bought him books, taken him to libraries, but had not had his friends over. Once, she had taken him to Coney Island, but the sight of his happiness in the water mixed with her memories of that place had hurt her. She had not taken him back. She had not taken him to a circus or a ball game or an ice rink. She had not provided him with a father to kick a ball with in the park.

She slept poorly, recalling, in the middle of the night, a cake Claire had once baked for her birthday—a sponge cake with cream and jam, the only birthday of hers that had ever been remembered. She woke to a watery winter light and a terrible silence in the apartment, and when she could no longer bear it, she rose and went out in the rain for the newspaper. She made coffee and read *The New York Times* at the table. A young heiress had been kidnapped—taken from her apartment in Berkeley. She turned the pages, read a review of a restaurant, gazed at photos of homes and gardens, and then, near the end, as if fate had cruelly decreed it that lonely morning, she turned a page to find David's smiling face, a radiant bride by his side, and underneath, a notice.

Bianca Rodriguez and David O'Hara were married in Holy Cross Church in Manhattan on December 29th, followed by a reception at the Tavern on the Green. The bride, 29, is the daughter of Mr. and Mrs. Pablo Rodriguez, Lima, Peru, and a senior stewardess with Pan Am Airlines. The bridegroom, 35, is an associate at the Manhattan law firm Goldberg and Levine, where he specializes in corporate law.

It was to Willa she turned. She stood in her friend's kitchen that evening and opened her purse and silently handed her the clipping. Willa was serving up the evening meal. She paused, read it, and, without uttering a word, went on ladling out food to her husband and children and Theo at the table. Then she touched Tess's arm lightly and got her coat. They walked along the street, their heads bent close. They sat in a diner until their coffee grew cold. Tess told her friend everything: the dead mother, the dead sister, the childhood, the man. In the telling it did not seem so bad. She even laughed at times. It was not that it was funny, but neither was it tragic. It was as if she were recounting someone else's life, from long ago.

12

One Sunday morning when he was fourteen he walked into the kitchen and stood before her.

"Who is my father?" he asked.

He stood still. She had rehearsed this moment many times before sleep. But she was not prepared for the iron grip that fastened on her heart now, the trapdoor she fell through. He would abandon her. He would enter a new life. He would enter a ready-made family with a house in the suburbs and a lawn and a pool and beautiful friends. She saw it all. An education too. He would reclaim the father she had deprived him of. She had done too little. She should have found his father, insisted he play his part.

"I will tell you his name when you are eighteen. I did not know him long, but I loved him. I cannot say if he loved me."

He held her look, then turned and left the room.

She had often, over the years, pored over the newspaper clipping of the wedding notice. They were both beautiful. The bride's exotic eyes, her lustrous hair, the groom's allure. Tess looked at her own pale freckled arms, her rural hands, and felt insignificant. She gazed at their faces, searched the bride's eyes, her confident pose, looked at her for a long time. Something began to take hold, and clarify. Slowly it came to her that this was the only kind of woman he could have chosen—sanguine, self-assured, with a center of her own. She would not want to climb behind his eyes or probe his silence or know its source. In that instant Tess saw their life together, his silence, her acceptance, and she felt a sudden gratitude to this woman, this stranger. She would let him be.

One night her aunt Molly passed away in her sleep. Tess and Fritz followed the coffin down the church aisle, and she and Theo rode with him in the funeral car out to Woodlawn Cemetery. She looked out at the streets and houses going by. She had been in the country for fifteen years, some tumultuous times. She had lost Claire and now Molly, her father and Mike Connolly were gone too, and she did not know where Oliver was. Her collection of mortuary cards was growing. She sent word of Molly's death home to Ireland. Her sisters' replies, in turn, offered condolences and glimpses of their own lives occupied with raising families and earning a living. Occasionally, on hearing that the Gallaghers or the O'Dowds or other Irish neighbors were making a visit back, Tess felt a little twinge. It was an ache for the place, more than for the people, and for a past that was bound to others, some now gone. She was not certain that a visit home would sate that ache, and year by year it grew harder to imagine a return.

Sometimes, in the months after Molly's passing, she longed for the nearness of a blood relative. She went down to 183rd Street to visit Fritz. He was sitting in his old chair, frail, drinking. He talked about Molly. Later she asked about Oliver. He searched and found Oliver's last known address. The next day she took the subway to Queens, to a brownstone boardinghouse and an Irish landlady who remembered him, remembered that he'd worked at the Ford plant in Jersey and on a construction site in Staten Island. That afternoon Tess stepped onto a building site in Staten Island, walked uneasily in the shadow of a great metal skeleton, amid noise and smells that reminded her of childhood and the new tar roads being laid. Under the gaze of male eyes, she spoke to the foreman, Tubridy. He had hired Oliver and would do so again, he said, if he turned up. He had not stayed long. He was a drinker. He was there one day and gone the next, and no sign of him ever since.

She walked away. She remembered warm evenings that first summer, walking downtown with him, this golden, blue-eyed brother, stopping to listen to the notes of a saxophone drifting out a window. He could be anywhere now. He could be happy. He could be dead. He might have opted to drop from the grid and disappear. This was America. As she walked along unfamiliar streets she wondered if the self she had become, and the self that Oliver had become, and the self that Claire had been, would have been any different if they'd had a mother who lived.

One day, cleaning, she found on top of her wardrobe a scroll of charts, handed to her at the school door one afternoon by Theo's fifth-grade teacher. It was not the words he had used that day— ordinary enough words of praise, and few—but the way he had hovered, and the look of earnestness, as if seeking a way to make her understand that his offering signified something.

She unrolled the charts now again, five, six of them. The Greek gods on Mount Olympus—with illustrations and carefully penned accounts of the twelve gods and goddesses—then, further down, the Wooden Horse at Troy, the Cyclops, Penelope. Other charts: the American War of Independence, its battles and heroes; the countries of Europe, color-coded in pastels, the demographic details boxed inside each country. She admired the neat handwriting, the perfect lines ruled in pencil. He had lain on his belly on the floor at night, writing, drawing, the TV volume turned low, the soft back-and-forth sound of his pencils as he shaded in. He had been ten then, and never happier.

Now, in his teenage years, there appeared to her a dulling, a dimming, of his natural curiosity, a diminution of his thirst for knowledge. He no longer read for pleasure. He spent his evenings in his room, lying on his bed, listening to music and staring at the ceiling. On Saturdays he worked in a record store, and he slept all day or stayed over with friends through Sundays. She could not broach her concerns. Conversations were sparse, and even minor inquiries about his day resulted in monosyllabic replies or sudden rebuffs that wounded her. His looks began to alter too. His face lost symmetry and proportion and refinement. His jaw jutted out, rough-hewn, giving him a raw unfinished look. His limbs, his gait, his whole bearing now seemed at odds with the boy she knew him to be. These changes were temporary, she knew, normal, and yet they left a disquiet in her, and one evening when he opened the refrigerator and the haunting white light crossed his face she was struck by the awful thought that he was growing gradually deformed before her eyes.

And then, little by little, year by year, his features settled and his face realigned, and he became complete. And she had been mistaken—there had been no diminution. His curiosity had simply narrowed, grown more focused, gathered inwards. Instead of its previous wide reach his hunger now had an intense clarity and concentration. She would find, strewn on his desk and on his bedroom floor, pages of calculation, mathematical equations, algebra. He made sense of it all. He could prove theorems, solve complex problems in trigonometry, calculus, his tiny figures like hieroglyphics. He could probe the mystery of infinite numbers. Her heart soared. He will be a scientist or an architect or an engineer, she thought. He will one day build a great bridge, or a fine house on a hill, ringed by cypresses and an air of gloom. She stood at his door one evening as he studied. He was hunched over his desk. She wished he were small again. On the window ledge a prism, a pyramid, a multicolored cube from his childhood.

"Dinner's ready . . . What're you at?" She longed to find a way back to him.

Without moving his head he prodded the cover of a textbook with his finger.

She hovered in the doorway. "I had no aptitude for math in school," she said. She shook her head in mock disbelief. "How do you do it, Theo, how do you understand all those symbols? It's beyond me—like a foreign language!"

He stared at her coldly. "Is it now? Beyond you? Ever think *you* might be beyond people? You—and your own fucking foreign language." He said each word slowly, brutally.

She could barely walk back to the kitchen.

The next evening he emerged from his room and did not speak, a book propped at the table as he ate. He had begun to judge her.

"His name is David," she said. "He's Irish too, from Dublin, but lives here . . . or did anyway. We met through mutual friends and had a brief . . . friendship . . . He joined the air force and I didn't hear from him. When you were born I wrote him and told him. I sent two letters. He never replied." She looked at him, waited. "He's a lawyer here, somewhere in the city. He's married now. You may have brothers and sisters."

He said nothing. His face was sullen, his chest rising and falling rapidly.

She got up and went to her bedroom and returned with the newspaper clipping, and left it by his plate.

"That's all I know, all I have," she said. "You have his name now. I do not know his date of birth or his address or anything else."

She let him read.

"One day you will want to find him," she said, distantly.

He asked no questions then or in the days following, or after. She told Willa.

"You did the right thing," Willa said softly. "It's hard, but the kid will survive. There are worse things than having no papa."

A long contemptuous silence ensued, times when he simmered, seethed, bristled at just the sight of her in the kitchen. It would have been easier if he'd kicked down doors. She left money and notes on the table, delayed her return from work in the evenings. On weekends he stayed out late, drinking. Her heart was breaking.

One Saturday morning before his graduation, a girl emerged from his room into the hall. She looked up, her hair touseled, a jacket in her hand, and saw Tess. Startled, the girl took a step towards the kitchen door.

"I'm sorry," she said. "I didn't know . . . I'm very sorry."

She was young, no more than sixteen, blond. Her voice was soft, kind, ashamed. Tess looked at her and a fear, an irrational mindless fear that had lain dormant in the far reaches of her mind, unearthed itself: that out there, somewhere in the city, Theo had sisters, brothers. They might live nearby. They might go to the same school, to the same bars and ball games. She could not speak or even nod to the girl. Rising from her mind was the image of her son naked, in the sexual act, rearing up on his sister.

In the following weeks a shift occurred, and a slight truce took hold. Small offerings were made. She found, on the table one evening, a school assignment, "The Golden Mean," scored with an A+. She leafed through the paper, pages with tables and columns of numbers, text too—the longest entitled "The Fibonacci Sequence." She read the overview, random paragraphs, the conclusion. She felt a surge of pride, and joy at his return, at the possibilities of his youth and all that lay before him.

There had been a time, briefly, in adolescence, when she had feared for him. He had frightened her with his subterranean silence, and a stare so deep she had felt imperiled. She would picture him at school slouched at his desk, distracted, perplexed, his eye scanning the text and then the air, as if searching for the equation for human feeling. And then interludes when his talk grew profuse, fragmented, euphoric, and he could not sleep. Everything—his whole being—disturbed by a storming of the spirit.

She felt his struggle, as if a part of him—some deep *Theo* part— yet needed begetting. Or was being begot. She waited for that part to be switched on, for the faint little bleeps to sound, and for him to come to. More than once her fear spiked into panic that what she was witnessing was the beginnings of mania, or a schizophrenic breakdown. She prayed. She made deals with God. She worried that he had been bequeathed something terrible by his father, which had lain latent within him until now. She wrestled with herself, feared that her flawed mothering had caused a rupture and unseated some deep psychological disturbance.

And then, in his late teens, the storm began to abate. Clipped by a demon, she thought. A darkness fell on him for weeks, as if he were grieving for an ancient fabulous self, mourning its loss at a deep cellular level, feeling the taming, the tempering, the toll it was taking to beget his mortal self and allow the entity that was Theo to emerge and live and move and have its being in the world.

13 It happened first one Sunday morning at Mass, and again, the next day, in line at the hospital cafeteria—the urge to touch a man. Any man, any man's hand, any man's arm. Or lean against a man, leave her head on his shoulder. In crowded places, in shops and buses, she had to fight the impulse to reach out. A face was not essential. The view from behind, the broad shoulders, the back of a head, a neck. A hirsute hand on a wallet, on a tray moving alongside her in the hospital cafeteria, could bring on the urge. Her fingers twitched and she longed to touch skin, lay her hands on a head, be privy to a man. One night at a retirement party for a colleague, she stood in the corner of the room watching people, couples, their body language, their secret signs. Her friend Priscilla was at one end of the room, her husband at the other. Tess saw him turn, find his wife. She saw the look they exchanged. Later at the bar he kissed the top of her head. She had an image of them driving home, whispering, giggling, as they undressed in the dark, their son sleeping in the next room. She looked around at all the wives. Did they realize their good fortune? How, at any moment, day or night, they could lie against their men, lay claim to them, lay their heads on chests, their hands on heads.

On the crowded subway a few days later a man seated next to

her accidentally touched her foot. He was wearing a light suit, navy blue, expensive. His beautiful hands rested on his legs. His left leg was partly touching hers. She felt the rise and fall of his breath. Under the fabric his thigh muscles flexed. Weak, she left her hands on her lap. The need to touch him was immense. The train curved, eased into a bend and her body leaned lightly against his. She closed her eyes, imagined him raising an arm, taking her into his wingspan. He shifted to free himself. Then the train was speeding into a station and he was on his feet, moving along the aisle. She rose and pushed through and stood behind him. He was poised to exit. Outside, on the platform, a million eyes, and the door opened with a hiss and, in the crush and split second that his body leaned forward, she put a hand on his arm and pressed her face into his back, and simultaneously closing her eyes and inhaling, she moved with him, in communion with him and with the body of passengers alighting from the train. *Pardon me.* Her voice was clipped, confident, her tone sincere, as if she had merely bumped him accidentally, absentmindedly, so preoccupied with life was she, and then carried on, stepping to the left when he went right, going, against her will, on her way.

On the platform, she stood, dazed. Out in the streets people pushed by her. She moved along the sidewalk, heat coming off the pavement. She looked up at the street numbers—she was in the 80s, far from home. She looked in gleaming shopwindows, cafés, restaurants with diners outside under awnings. The sun beat down. She crossed onto quieter streets. Fine hotels, apartment buildings with doormen. She looked up at the windows. She saw, in her mind's eye, lovers in shaded rooms, naked, spent. Emerging out onto the street later, holding hands, all loved up. *All loved up.* Those were the words Willa had used one time telling a story when she and Darius had returned from a vacation. *There we were*, she'd said, *heading out for dinner, all loved up.*

She turned right, crossed Third Avenue, then Second, First,

York, drawn by the promise of water. She entered a park and followed the path. Families with children, young couples, old men
with dogs and sorrowful eyes seeking the shade of trees. Then
she was standing on the edge of the East River. Seagulls' wings
glinted in the sun. On the other side, in a blue haze, Queens. It
was there he had lived. A boat passed and left behind a trail of
white foam. She watched it spread and diffuse, until there was
almost no trace left. Watching the swell and motion of the waves
and the surf, she felt seasick. She tried not to break. She looked
around. Under the still surface of the day she saw turmoil everywhere. She thought of the water that had lain quietly calm, each
tiny drop, each molecule, restful, suddenly wrenched, catapulted
through a metal rotary, tossed back out into the turbulent cur-
rent, reeling, confounded, changed.

She confessed her compulsion to Willa. They were sitting under
trees in Inwood Hill Park, behind them a hill of old stone, like a
quarry. They had brought a small picnic, and wine.

"I think there's something wrong with me. I've started looking at men, strange men," she said shyly.

Willa eyed her, beamed a smile. "Go on!"

She winced. "On the subway, in church, you know, just
watching them . . . I can't help myself. It's turning into an obses-
sion. Next I'll be stalking them!"

"Oh, Tess, you're just a real ripe healthy woman, that's all!"
She gave a little smile. "We'll have to find you a suitor, Miss
Lohan. We'll have to find you some gorgeous gentleman caller!"

She expected Theo to enter a field of science, or the humanities.
She thought this was where his sensibilities lay. But he chose

business at Fordham College. For a time he continued to live with her, before moving into a house in Harlem with a girlfriend and two friends. He took all his belongings, his records. She did not think he would ever come back. Little by little, since childhood, he had grown further from her. She wondered if he had ever searched for his father. He called her each Friday; their conversations centered on his studies and finances. Now and then he dropped by. In person he gave off an air of irritation. She felt estranged from him. She felt his resistance to being fully known by her, as if time spent together in naked silence would reveal something he could not bear. And yet, at times, she saw understanding in his eyes. When he rose to leave, a softening occurred, a hesitation in his limbs. She knew then that he had gleaned the parting sickness in her. She felt the terrible tug and conflict within him and wanted to free him. In that moment she braced herself, summoned all her strength, affected an air of busyness, of a life fully engaged, and sent him on his way. Her rooms could barely endure the silence left in his wake.

No gentleman caller wooed her. Some tried, but no love materialized. She went on several hopeful dates with Priscilla's brother-in-law, a high school teacher, a great bear of a man whose ebullience and overeagerness to please ate up all her energy. She began to see an older man, a doctor at the hospital—a divorcé. He took her to an elegant restaurant and with a little wine inside her she felt beautiful, and in the candlelight he was not unhandsome. His manners were impeccable. He had just returned from Rome. But in his hands, in his darting eyes and self-conscious awareness of himself in the world, she sensed an otherness, felt him a stranger. She knew already he was not a fit. In her life, ever, there were only a few people who had been a fit, with whom she had felt understood. Her mother, Claire, David, Willa. In his childhood, Theo. The longing to be with them persisted, a longing so deep and eternal it must have had ancient origins.

Out in the street her doctor hailed a cab. "May I kiss you?" he asked.

She smiled. "I haven't been kissed in quite a while."

"All the more reason to kiss you then." He drew her to the shadows. He was a man used to getting his own way. He took her face in his hands and kissed her and paused, until she kissed him back. The kisses grew longer and with the wine and his hands moving on her back she felt herself yielding, arching into him, her body egging her on. When they drew apart he was smiling. He seemed bemused, triumphant, arrogant. He became, again, strange to her. His face did not move her. There was little in him she wanted to know.

"Till next time, then," he said.

Inside the cab she could smell his cologne. She closed her eyes and laid her head back. She longed for a passionate, even outrageous, life. She pictured him naked, rutting. His hands on her, all over her, in her. Strange hands, strange eyes. And his mind, his thoughts, alien too, and so apart from hers. She opened her eyes. She could not give herself to this stranger. She would need to be *known*. She would need to know him too, decipher him, make unstrange his mind. She would need to be a little in love. And this man—a divorcé and a man of the world—would not wait. This was the way with men.

In the days following she tried to want him—she wanted to want him. But in her private fantasies she could not call him forth. It was David who came, always David, his face known to her, his voice tender and lonely, his mind adhered to hers. They had come together once, like planets colliding. Her body had never forgotten him, not for an instant, as if by being her first, by taking and entering and impregnating her, he had annexed her, and some twist or quirk of nature had ensured that he remain. Her Adam, her primary man, the first and foremost, the father, the one who had made his mark and against whom all others would be measured.

Frustrated, impatient, she vowed to sublimate desire. She turned to learning. She had always considered herself an unlettered woman but resolved to cultivate a life of the mind. Theo's legacy, the fire of his passion and early curiosity, was igniting in her now. She enrolled in an evening class on Greek mythology at the library a few blocks away on Broadway. From the start, she was intoxicated. Alone, she wept for Demeter's grief, for Prometheus's torment as he lay bound to the rock. The gods and goddesses entered her and resonated, and she was porous to every myth and odyssey, as if the ghosts of Olympus had always lain dormant in her, waiting to be resurrected. She encountered them everywhere, found them threaded through her days, in ads and logos, in films, on the signage of trucks, in the names of towns—Troy, Ithaca, Delphi Falls. Ancient Greece was all over America. On street corners she saw people descend into the subway, and felt a little shiver at their blind oblivion, had an urge to forewarn them, hand them coins, beseech them not to look back.

She relayed the tales back to Willa—each week returning with books, reading aloud passages that told of the antics of Zeus and Apollo and Aphrodite, so that Willa too was drawn in, playfully taking sides, expressing faux outrage and delight, bringing a new way of seeing to Tess.

"He's a piece of work, that Zeus!" Willa said. "Now Hera—she's my kind of woman. If my Zeus ever, *ever* strayed, I tell you, hon, Hera's got nothing on me in the jealousy department! My Darius—you know he's named for a king?" She paused. "*Darius, King of Persia.*" She smiled, as if a gentle memory had surfaced.

"But, king or no king . . ." She sighed, shook her head. "Oh, Tess, it ain't love if it ain't jealous."

How odd they must look, two women in their forties, one black, one white, sitting in the park, or walking home along the streets, sharing mythological aches, trying to outwit each other with priapic puns.

"So, which crazy god has put a stamp on you, Miss Lohan?" They were sitting in Willa's apartment, by the open window, drinking iced tea. Willa's sons were grown up now too, and working; one a policeman, already married.

Tess thought. "Mmm . . . probably Persephone." The sun was streaming in. She remembered a picture of Hades in his chariot, and the ground cleaving open as the chariot and team of horses dived underground with the captive girl, crying. "Or maybe Orpheus."

"No, you've got to pick a girl."

"Eurydice then." She remembered Orpheus's grief, ascending from the Underworld without his beloved.

Willa shook her head. "You're *obsessed* with the Underworld."

Her voice trailed off. She turned towards the light, and Tess was caught by her sudden calm and poise, the tilt of her face, and her eyes, in that instant, a little melancholy. A small tendril of hair curled in on her temple. The smooth curve of her neck gleaming with the heat, her small wrists, her slender fingers— all of her familiar and beautiful, and now unexpectedly sensual. Tess's heart pounded. She looked away. The lace curtain lifted in the breeze. In the distance the city hummed. A silence fell and Tess looked at her friend again and something stirred in her and she could not tear her eyes away. The white collarless blouse, almost see-through, rested on her collarbone. Underneath, her skin, her breasts. There was something infinitely tender, infinitely delicate, about the small mound of each breast, the thin filmy cloth like a veil over them. She had a sudden longing to reach out, move aside the fabric, touch a breast, lay her head there, her mouth, ease her terrible ache for human touch, human love. The room was flooded with light and she was blinded, mesmerized. Scarcely breathing, she raised her eyes to Willa's face, and they held each other's look. Then Willa stood and moved away. Tess placed her hands flat on her lap and closed her eyes and came to her senses. She had almost lost her mind. She had almost lost the run of herself.

The evenings of that first winter alone, and of the winters following, had a denser darkness. In the streets she was assailed by glances, light strobes, flashing neon lights. Her working days grounded her. She was grateful for the comfort of routine, the rhythm of each day with its journey, its duties, the small news and gossip of other nurses' lives.

Occasionally she thought about retiring, moving house, taking a trip back to Ireland, but she did none of these things. There was in her nature a certain passivity, an acquiescence that was ill-suited to change or transformation, as if she feared ruffling fate or rousing to anger some capricious creature that lay sleeping at the bottom of her soul.

Theo had long since separated from her, and when his college education was complete he pulled up the drawbridge to his inner life, locked his heart against her. He had been a fatherless boy and now he was a man, and she accepted this, and understood. He went to work for a firm in the city, and year after year advanced in his field. A gambler of sorts, he explained, trading commodities, buying and selling gold, silver, rice, soybeans. "Coffee beans too," he said, picking up the coffee can in her kitchen one day. An image of Africa formed—of Kenya, and Isak Dinesen, and Robert Redford washing Meryl Streep's hair in a film she'd seen, Meryl's head back, the water falling from the jug onto her hair, sparkling in the sun. That night they danced outside the tent. She remembered the music, clearly. Lately she'd been doing this, slipping into reverie or something that resembled reverie.

She looked up at Theo. "How tall are you?" She herself was growing down. He half smiled. "Six foot two. You know that. Why?" She had known. Since he was a teenager and had played basketball, she had known. She did not know why she asked. She remembered buying razors when she saw the first tufts of facial hair, leaving them in the bathroom for him to find.

When he was twenty-eight he became engaged to a tall Jewish girl named Jennifer, a lawyer, who sometimes accompanied him now on his visits to Tess. A perfect couple, both blond, both beautiful. They bought an apartment on Riverside Drive. He was closer now to the girl than to anyone, ever, in his whole life. Before the wedding they took Tess to meet her parents and friends at a country club in Westchester County. Out on the lawn she watched Theo moving among them. She saw his ease, the way they embraced him, appropriated him. She could no longer hug him or kiss his head. To touch an arm was the extent of what she could do. All evening long she smiled and mingled, but she felt remote. It seemed at times that she was marooned on an island, a moat of water, wide and black, separating her from all human love. She thought of Claire, years ago, and her house and garden in New Jersey, and how all things change or end or disappear, and this would too, this day, this moment. She looked around. *And you too, you will all disappear.*

She returned home after midnight. She stepped inside and stood still, alone again. She had left the radio on all day. Others had people waiting. She took off her shoes and poured herself a glass of wine and sat at the kitchen table. He had been long gone but now the going was complete. She had sent him out of her house into his fate and he had grown and succeeded and become unknowable to her. She wanted to cry out, roll on the floor. She had loved him wrongly. She had become too attached. She should not have grafted herself onto him. She made a fist of her hand and bit on her knuckles. There was nothing before her now. He belonged to someone else. She remembered the couples at a party years ago, the looks, the trust, the secret signs, and a rage— an unbearable pain—pierced her and she let out a howl and flung her glass across the kitchen, hard against the wall, and cried as the wine ran down, sudden and fast, in thin purple rivulets until it reached the skirting board and then parted and flowed right and left and over the top onto the floor.

She walked out into the night. The streets were warm, quiet, almost tropical. Under the sky there was nothing, no one to cling to. The paucity of her life made her unspeakably sad. She tried to put her finger on what had marred her, what had excluded her from life. Again she began to cry. What she had longed for was to be of one mind with someone. Of one mind and one body. *Love.* She walked along the edge of the park. Ahead of her, nothing but this longing, this sickness, this time.

She walked along Sherman Avenue, Broadway. She felt calmer. There was something about walking, steps unwinding out of the body, that brought comfort and clarity. Was there not something in her that secretly savored this state of longing? Waiting with constant hope and everything before her, all to play for? Was not the ache sweeter, in a way, more enticing, more seductive, than the sating? Like waiting for the afterlife, she thought, but never truly wanting it to arrive. Because then, what would be left? It would spell the death of hope in the everyday, like love born dead.

She stopped outside the church, its great wooden doors locked. Its stone walls hinted at further silence and sympathy within. And then the night stood still and she looked up at the stars. A serene peace entered her, and her heart lifted and it came to her with the clarity of a vision: Theo had love. He was in love, and loved, and beloved. He was understood. And in the better part of herself she knew this was all that mattered.

In the better part of herself. Had she not glimpsed beauty? Had she not, at times, felt blessed? Had she not felt the surge and soar of love, the glint of grace and, once, had not the planets collided, and had she not burned with passion? Love *had* existed, she had felt its throb, its inner vibration. Even if, on that night, their carnal bodies had not bestowed beauty on the act itself. But it had existed. Had not a child come out of it and been delivered fully fledged to the world? Images from the past returned to her: entering Willa's apartment in the evenings, the child running into her arms, making her heart leap in her breast. To give joy like that. To see him sitting in his bath, eyes closed, laughing, as she rinsed his hair and the warm water trickled down his face. Or lying on the floor drawing men on the moon, animals marching in pairs onto Noah's Ark, asking her to spell a word, and she, she, in the wash of him, feeling the truth of him deep in her soul.

She walked on home. She moved with divine calm, as if all the world were sleeping. She remembered a line from a book: *For the beautiful word begets the beautiful deed*, and felt vast, deep, complete.

Part Three

14 Over the years, over long winter nights and summer afternoons, Tess found a new life in books. As if possessed of a homing instinct, she would often leave her hand on a title on a library shelf or in a bin outside a bookstore that somehow magically fitted her at that moment. The mere sighting of a book on her hall table or nightstand as she walked by, the author's name or title on the spine, the remembrance of the character—his trials, his adversity—took her out of ordinary time and induced in her an intensity of feeling, a sense of union with that writer. Another vocation, then, reading, akin even to falling in love, she thought, stirring, as it did, the kind of strong emotions and extreme feelings she desired, feelings of innocence and longing that returned her to those vaguely perfect states she had experienced as a child. She was of the mind now that this evocation, this kind of dream living was sufficient, and perhaps, in its perfection, preferable to the feeble hopes embedded in reality.

The things she had hankered after—encounters with beauty, love, sometimes the numinous—she found in books. She flinched from the ugly, the vulgar, but never from suffering or the pain of shame, discerning in the author's soul a striving to transcend these states, to draw out of injury or anguish some revelation, some insight, that would deliver both character and reader into a new state of grace. She suffered for the characters, for the authors too. She lived in a divided world, the inner at a remove from the outer other. It was this inner alter-life that rendered her outer life significant and in which she felt most exquisitely contained. She became herself, her most true self, in those hours among books. I am made for this, she thought. In the shade of a tree a bird would call and she would lift her head from her novel, arrested, heart-weakened. Then she would remove her glasses and come to, up out of a trance and into the world where joggers and schoolchildren and old couples linking arms drifted in shade and mottled light, a world that newly bedazzled her.

It was not that she found in novels answers or consolations but a degree of fellow feeling that she had not encountered elsewhere, one that left her feeling less alone. Or more strongly alone, as if something of herself—her solitary self—was at hand, waiting to be incarnated. The thought that once, someone—a stranger writing at a desk—had known what she knew, and had felt what she felt in her living heart, affirmed and fortified her. He is like me, she thought. He shares my sensations.

There did not seem to be enough hours or days or years left in her life to read all she wanted to read. She moved about the world with gratitude, porous to beauty and truth. At Mass she felt a new appreciation for the Scriptures, the gospels, the sounds of the Psalms. She went to certain Masses, certain churches, for the music alone, to be exalted. She attended recitals, listened to radio concerts. It was as if she had undergone a tenderizing of the heart, a refinement of the soul, with everything reaching her at a pure and distinct register.

She went out to dinner occasionally, and to concerts, with Willa or Priscilla. Theo and Jennifer took her out for her birthday and at other random times. Two years into their marriage Jennifer gave birth to a son, Alex, and a year later to a daughter, Rachel. At the first sight of each grandchild she had been profoundly moved. Her very flesh and blood were there before her. It was miraculous. She had a new sense of her place in the world, of a continuum. She thought that Theo, if he had not already done so, might now seek out his own father, and was torn between curiosity and mild dread at the prospect of such news.

When she was sixty-two she retired from her job at the hospital and moved from her apartment on Academy Street into a building with an elevator, thirty blocks south. Before she left, she received from Willa a farewell gift, a kitten. At the last minute in her old kitchen the two women embraced. She thought of how something in Willa always helped constellate Tess's better self. She remembered the moment of overpowering sensuality she'd felt in Willa's kitchen years before. There had been that moment, and no more, the instinct never awoken again. And no fear, no struggle, no shame. This was, Tess knew, in part to do with Willa, with her ease, her serene understanding of all human matters. The love was implicit. And she knew, if she had ever broached the subject, what Willa would have said. *Oh, honey, when it comes to the heart, it ain't about men or women, but people.*

Her new apartment was on a quiet street in the 170s, not far from her aunt Molly's old home. The residents were older, more sedate, than those on Academy Street. There was a school at the end of the street, and through her open window she heard the cries of children in the playground. She named the kitten Monkey, because of his antics. She began to talk to him. She did not like to leave him alone for long. She let him sleep on her bed, waking early to his soft purr vibrating against her temple. Sometimes she kissed him. She had not known such reward could come from so insignificant a being.

In the early years of her grandchildren's lives she experienced sudden frequent longings to see them, but a natural reserve—and the fear of becoming a nuisance—prevented her from ever visiting, uninvited, her son and his wife. She attended birthday parties and Thanksgivings at their home but otherwise she did not think she had the right to ask. Occasionally, out of the blue, Theo would drop by with the children. Her bell would buzz and then, his voice. *Hi, Mom.* Her heart leapt at the thought of his face, the thought of the children. She bought them toys, clothes, books. She, in turn, received a steady stream of gifts, more than she'd ever received in her whole life—sweaters, scarves, books, and, once, a stereo sound system, which brought a new dimension and richness to her life. On weekend nights, she put on her music, cooked and ate her dinner, and drank a glass of red wine, content. The image of Theo setting up the speakers in her living room often returned to her. And the image of him in a store, choosing the system for her. *Giving her thought.* For a few minutes, for a specific time, he had given her thought. At times, a gap of several weeks would open during which she did not hear from him. She felt very unsure of her place in his life then, assuming that, in the midst of his and Jennifer's busy routines, they had forgotten her. She had always felt separate from people, and lately she had the sense that when she was out of view she disappeared entirely from the minds of others. At such moments she siphoned off images from the past and used them to imagine herself back into existence.

"The King of Persia is dying. Oh, Tess . . . what am I going to do?"
She was back in her old neighborhood, in the diner she and

Willa had often sat in when the children were small. Now, together, they cried. "Lung cancer. From those damn cigarettes . . . and all those years in his underground train. It's not natural, that . . ." She shook her head. "A subterranean man—that's what Darius was." She looked at Tess. "Six months, they said. Oh, Tess."

She put an arm around her friend. She called up words to give hope. She cited new treatments, cases she'd known in the hospital that had turned out well. Willa shook her head. "No, Tess, it's not good. I just know." She closed her eyes and sighed. "I've known him so long—since I was sixteen years old. We never spent a night apart, except when I was giving birth." She looked out the window onto the street. "How will I go on living without him?"

In the library on 179th Street, one evening in September, she found a slim book of poetry. On the front cover there was a portrait of a man with fixed haunted eyes. Years before, she had thought poetry beyond her. She read the biographical note and the introduction. Then page after page—sonnets for Orpheus, the raising of Lazarus, a requiem. Her deepest nerves were touched, sudden mysteries given sanction. Outside, the light began to fade. She looked up and out of the high window. If I could just live here eternally, she thought, at this desk, in this light, with this poem. The librarian touched her arm, whispered, "Time." She checked out the book and stepped onto the street. Under the twilight the lines repeated themselves. *Who, if I cried, would hear me among the angelic orders?* She walked to their beat, the words in harmony with her feet, her feet in harmony with her heart.

Something brushed her arm, pressed against her. She felt a jolt and looked up. She had strayed onto the wrong street. A shadow darkened over her, and faces, all black, closed in on hers.

Teenage boys loomed above her, bearing down on her. An open mouth, teeth close up to her face, roaring obscenities. She tried to speak. Cold eyes glared at her and she shrank backwards, another body, like a wall, behind her. Then her arm was tugged and her bag wrenched. No, she begged, my book. She held fast to the strap. *Bitch.* A violent tug and she lost her footing, and as she went down she saw a boot, black, high, being raised. She put her hands to her face and covered her head. She waited. And then it came, not a blow to the head or the stomach, but a boot on the small of her back, left there for a long moment, and then pressed. She held her breath, numb, until she heard footsteps running away.

A man and a woman knelt beside her. The woman dialed her cell phone. Trembling, Tess began to rise. *Stay, stay*, they urged. She pushed herself onto her knees, rose, and fled. She lurched to the right, then left, along the sidewalk, lost. She looked up, searching for signs, landmarks. At a corner she halted, traffic whizzing by. She stepped to the edge of the curb and raised a feeble hand and hailed a cab.

Willa took her to the hospital, stayed for the X-rays, took her home again, remained with her through the night as she drifted in and out of sleep. She heard a foghorn in the distance, dreamt of ships, rain, a burning bush. In the morning she stood before the bathroom mirror and cried.

All day she slept. In the evening Theo came. When he entered the room she struggled to sit up. "Shh," he whispered. "Go back to sleep."

She lay back. In the faint glow of the night light they were silent. She felt his presence, mightily, in the room.

"I've been lying here . . . thinking," she said. She could not look at him. "There's so much I regret, so much I wish I'd done differently."

They were silent for a long time.

"I wanted a strong mother," he said. "Like Mary O'Dowd.

Or Willa." He was speaking into the dark. "I had no father and . . . you were always so . . . afraid."

He sounded wounded, like an injured animal.

"You were all I had," she said, pleading. "I did my best."

She began to cry. He stroked her arm for the first time.

"Shh, don't cry . . . I didn't understand then. I was only a kid. I didn't know anything . . . and you never talked much. We never talked much."

"We can talk now."

He shrugged, looked away. The past flooded back. She brightened.

"You know, I think I got you wrong," she said. "I *thought* I knew you. For instance, I always thought you'd choose a career—a life—in the arts, or science. You were so creative when you were a child. And then you chose business!" She was smiling at him, like he was a child again. "Does it suit you? Do you like it?"

Again he shrugged, but softer. "I buy and sell. It's not really business as such . . . I deal in risk. Chance. The mathematics of chance. Yes, I like it."

"Once, years ago at a PTA meeting, your math teacher said you could solve problems without being taught."

He smiled. "I never understood why the others couldn't! I don't know . . . I probably got those things intuitively. You see . . . there's such logic and truth in math. And beauty. People don't see the beauty. They don't know that actually it's in math that beauty is *told*."

She loved to hear him talk like this. "What do you mean? How? How is beauty told?"

He searched, for a moment. "Let's take risk, chance. In math it's probability. In probability truth is clearly told. The beauty of probability is that truth, however vague, is logical. One outcome that is possible out of so many *happens*. People are amazed by that! Amazed by that chance. But why shouldn't it? In the very long run everything happens. Everything is inevitable."

The night grew dense around them. She drifted in and out of sleep. When she opened her eyes he was still there, in the chair.

"What time is it?" Her voice was young, like that of a girl. She remembered nights long ago, waking up when someone tiptoed into her room for something. He whispered a gentle reply. He was like a father now, watching over her.

Hours passed. In the dead of night she woke with a start, feverish, sweating. He was still there.

"Did you ever find him? Your father."

He looked into her eyes, and nodded.

"When?"

"A few years ago."

There were so many questions. The enormity of everything, of Theo's life, hit her.

"How will you ever forgive me?" she whispered.

The silence deepened. She could feel him recall it all. He leaned forward, his arms on his knees, his head down, and she grew afraid. When he lifted his head his face was soft, lighted.

"You're my mother," he said. "It's easy to forgive a mother."

She sank back on the pillow. He got up and took off his shoes and lay down on the bedcovers beside her. "Shh, go back to sleep now. We'll talk tomorrow." She did not know if she was dreaming or living this moment. She closed her eyes. She felt his breath on her face, sweet, the promise of peace. He left his hand on hers. The night drained away and the whole world slept.

In the morning he was gone. Monkey was in his chair. He had left a glass of orange juice on the nightstand beside her. She listened out for sounds in the corridor, for the ping of the elevator.

She got up, fed Monkey, walked around the apartment. The building was eerily quiet. She was besieged by loneliness. She wished she were back on Academy Street, hearing doors slam, shouting in the corridors. In the kitchen she tried to be busy. She made coffee and sat at the table. The minutes passed slowly. She felt old and alone, the years yawning before her, a graceless old woman with sagging flesh and clammy skin. A woman in decline. There was nothing to be done about it. Tomorrow would be the same.

Monkey jumped onto her lap and settled down and began to purr. She stroked the little head, cupped the tiny face in her hand. Poor little creature, she said. The eyes looked into hers, clear, green, shining. Theo was right. She had been too afraid. She had always been waiting for something to take, for the veils of abstraction to lift and reveal the life that was meant for her. There was a time, when Theo was small, when she thought *he* had cured her. He had been enough.

She grew distraught. He would forget what had occurred in the room last night. There would be no breakthrough. He would be his usual self the next time, and she would wonder if she had dreamt it. It was impossible to know the truth. So many feelings between people were encoded in gesture and silence, because words fell short. A time might come when words would be extinct and all communication conducted in silence. The line between sound and silence might simply dissolve.

A time might come. *A time might come.* A feeling of foreboding began to rise. She had the clear, distinct thought that something was wrong. She put a hand on her heart. She took her pulse. She touched each breast, pressing, searching, self-examining for lumps.

Willa came later. "It's normal to feel this way, Tess," she told her, "after what you've been through, the attack. You're not going to die! You've come through worse." She set down a cooked dinner before Tess.

"How is Darius?" She needed to remember others now.

Willa sighed. "We took a little walk this morning. The boys carried him downstairs in a chair."

Tess thought of all that was before Willa. We could set up house, you and I, she thought, like two spinster sisters. Care for each other, call to each other when we're frightened in the night.

That night she barely slept. At dawn she dozed off. Later, she woke to the phone ringing by her head. A cheery male voice tried to sell her a multichannel TV upgrade. She hung up and left the phone off the hook. The tone hummed on, then died. She got out and opened the window blind. A brilliant sky this morning, pure blue, without blemish. She hoped Theo would come again. She knew now there were only a few moments, ever, in one's life, when one is understood. She remembered a novel she had read. Michael K, a silent disfigured man wheeling his sick mother out of the city on a makeshift wheelbarrow and, after her death, wandering the desert, surviving on almost nothing. His mind growing emptier by the day. She had worried for him, as if he were real and in her life. She would have liked to have him as a son, have him mind her, mourn her.

She was living too much among books and memories, and this room had become a sickroom. She would go out later to the food store, the library. The day would herald a return. She would sit in her favorite café and eat a toasted English muffin with black-currant jelly. But first, she would sleep. She got back into bed. As soon as she lay down, yesterday's pall returned. She felt herself floating close to hazard. A vague intimation, a premonition, that there was more to come, that the end was nigh, and she would soon die. She leaned out and opened a drawer and took two sleeping pills and a mouthful of orange juice. Then she lay back.

A medley of sounds mingled with her dreams. Distant traffic, banging doors, her name being called. She was standing on a corner downtown. A voice behind her said "Look!" and she looked up and saw water—a circular shower amid the sun, with thick glistening drops enclosed in tiny membranes, and she was transfixed by their beauty. Then someone laughed and she turned, thinking they were laughing at her, frightened that she had lost her mind. Above it all she heard the sea.

She woke to a terrible gloom, and a knocking on the door. She was drunk with sleep. The air was dense and stale, the heat of the afternoon weighing down the room. Outside, the sky was still blue. She felt someone in the apartment, footsteps in the hall, voices. Alarmed, she tried to rise.

Willa stood in the bedroom doorway, the super beside her. Her face was solemn.

"Darius," Tess said. Willa shook her head, frowned, came and sat on the bed.

"Willa, you're frightening me. Please, what's wrong?" Her mind was slow, leaden. She looked at the super. She thought there was something she was missing.

Willa took her hands, looked into her eyes. "Have you seen the news, the TV?" Vaguely she shook her head. A wave of nausea began to rise in her. "*Theo*," she whispered.

The worst thing had finally happened, the calamity she had always been waiting for. It was almost a relief when it arrived, and the waiting was over. She felt a strange surreal calm sitting in front of the TV all evening. Over and over she watched two planes with glinting wings fly into skyscrapers, from a sky so blue it did not look real. Then the skyscrapers buckling, collapsing, folding under. People on the streets, their hands on their mouths, looking up in disbelief. People fleeing, enveloped in ash, as rivers of smoke pursued them through the streets. Everyone running, the cameras running, crowds crossing bridges, getting off the island. She wanted to go out and search but they would not allow it. She could not take her eyes from the screen. She saw them all running. And over and over the planes flying, the towers tumbling, the ground giving.

If she could die herself, then, at that moment, it would be all right. It would, actually, be the most perfect thing. She had always felt temporary, provisional, as if waiting in a holding bay. Now the wait was over. This thought brought peace. She wanted to hold this thought, this peace, but people kept entering the room, bending, speaking, touching her. All evening long they came. Some of them cried. The phones were down. Willa's sons came, then went out to join the search. She heard the elevator ping and her heart lifted and she turned her head and waited for him to enter. She got a towel, ready to wipe his face, wash his feet. She fetched her purse, urgent. What had she been thinking? Ludicrous, to think he would come here! He would go home to Academy Street, expecting to find her there. Gently, Willa led her back from the door. "Let's wait, Tess. Let's wait for some word. We have to be patient. We have to have hope."

Jennifer arrived, pale and distraught, with her brother. She hugged Tess. Theo had called her—he had talked to her from the stairwell between the 77th and 76th floors. She was certain he was out there.

After midnight she sent them all home, Willa too. She switched off the TV and listened to the silence. She stood at the sink and looked out at the night. *They have pierced my hands and my feet*, she whispered, *they have numbered all my bones*.

15

Dawn was the cruelest hour. The wind was sifting his bones, scattering his ash, leaving tiny pale shards in hidden corners. She wanted to roam the streets, scavenge in the sewers for his teeth. She sat at the table and tallied up his time: thirty-seven years, two months, and twenty-one days. Monkey kept meowing. "Stop that racket," she snapped. Then the elevator pinged. She tilted her head. "Is that you, Theo?"

People came by. Jennifer brought the children, but in their presence, especially the boy's, she felt inexplicably angry, and then, when they were gone, more deeply alone.

She was better at night. In the quiet apartment she fell under the spell of memories, dreams, visions. He was lying on the floor at her feet, drawing stars, his head in his hand, his heart on the floor. Oh, to be that floor. *Tell me their names, Theo, their constellations. Read me your favorite lines.* She closed her eyes. She was waiting, with others, at a gate. She could see him inside, seated at the right hand of his father. She tried to break away, run across the threshold into his arms, but a hand held her back. She was running through smoldering streets then, gathering up his bones, placing them in a little casket, bringing them home.

Monkey kept pestering her, breaking the spell. He jumped on her bed and rolled over, flagrant. She stroked his head, his pixie face. She caressed his belly, felt his heartbeat, his pulsing purr. With her fingers she encircled his neck . . . Such a small neck, all said. She pressed lightly. With my giant hands I could throttle you, she thought. I could crush your bones, see your eyes open wide with surprise, your sad little head slump over. He looked into her eyes. "Yes, you," she whispered. She placed her thumbs on his throat and pressed, and he meowed and lashed out and fled.

Days passed, then weeks. The grief was so deep her eyes could not weep. All good had gone out of the world. And to think that the world still went on. She saw again children playing, people eating and drinking and laughing, the purchase of life. Birds, books, the notes of a cello, the glossy green heads of ducks in a pond, all indifferent. She put the TV on mute, watched a man on a dust track in India, with trees, water, the setting sun— a huge orange orb lowering itself into the earth. She had never understood that—why the sun and the moon looked so large and near in the East. Intolerably beautiful. She had no armor left. She had no son left. Was there something she had missed? She stared at his photograph. Was there something she could have done to avert it? But the dead don't talk back. The dead don't talk. *The dead.*

On a cold bright Saturday in October, a funeral car collected her for the Memorial Mass. She climbed into the back and embraced Jennifer and the children. She stroked the children's heads. An image from the past rose up—a boy, a president's son, stepping forward to salute his father's casket.

"How are you holding up, Tess?" Jennifer asked tenderly.

She had succeeded in keeping feeling at bay all morning.

"Some days are better than others. You know yourself. When you wake up . . ."

"I do."

"Everyone is saying we're all in this together, united in our grief. But . . ." She frowned, shook her head.

"I know. It's so hard. I don't want anyone to be part of this either, except you and the children."

Tess began to cry.

Rachel's hair was plaited. She stroked the plaits. The child nestled against her.

"Tess," Jennifer said. "He never got to tell you. He made contact with his father. About three years ago, he found him."

"He told me. The night before he . . . The night he stayed over."

Jennifer reached across, touched her hand. "They met only once."

An image crossed her mind, a meeting in a café, an assignation. Momentarily, she felt deceived. "Does he know?"

"Yes. I called him."

She looked out the tinted glass window. *Your son is dead. Our son is dead.*

"They have no children—he and his wife," Jennifer said.

She left her hands flat each side of her on the seat. The smell of the polished leather was overpowering. Why must everything floor her so?

"Can you braid hair, Nana—do you know how?" Rachel was looking at her.

She smiled at the child. "Yes, sweetheart, I can braid hair. How about I teach you next time you come by? My sister taught me when I was small. Her name was Claire." She said it again, abstractedly. "Her name was Claire."

They pulled up at the Church of the Good Shepherd. She looked up at the steps, the three arched doorways. People from the old neighborhood stood outside, come to pay their respects, Willa among them.

She held on to the handrail as she climbed the steps. "Will he be here?" she asked in a low voice.

Jennifer leaned in, whispered, "No, don't worry."

In the middle of Mass, for some reason, she remembered that he was left-handed. Theo had inherited this trait. As a toddler she had watched it emerge, become manifest in an almost imperceptible pause, a faltering, before a hand reached out to a toy, as if a brief internal tussle was being played out, a faint quarrel between the two sides of him. In that pause, she intuited a shy soul, a vulnerability, a tender wound at the source, a little wrong that his little body was trying to right. "*We need, in love, to practice only one thing—letting go,*" the priest said and looked vaguely upwards, as if an invisible Theo was departing skywards before them. "God speed you," he added then. She had an image of birds in flight, a tunnel of light, the number Phi.

After Communion, *Esurientes.* The Magnificat. She had requested it. *Anima mea Dominum.* Her conversation with God. She tried to recover him, his hands, his sleeping eyes, but he would not be summoned. She could not conjure his face in death. The words and the music engulfed her. She rode on waves, lost, blind, awash in silent grief. She wanted to relish the pain, the sorrow in her marrow, the dark heart taking over. *Suscepit Israel puerum suum.*

She did not want it to end. When the choir began the final hymn the parting sickness rose in her. *The strife is o'er, the battle done.*

At a reception back at Theo's house, catering staff in white gloves moved among the mourners, pouring wine, bringing offerings on trays. She chose a morsel and chewed it but it lodged drily in her esophagus. She shook hands with strangers and semi-strangers.

She noted their pressed suits, their painted nails. Jennifer was the chief mourner. She heard their stories, laughter, memories of him. She heard them say his name. They had known him for five minutes, all of them, Jennifer too. It was in Tess that images of him dwelt, millions of them. *I am his mother*, she wanted to cry. *I made him. Inside me. With only a drop from a man now barely remembered I forged him, I molded him, body and soul.* She watched their mouths, their moving tongues, eating, speaking, their white teeth. How can you eat, she thought, at a time like this? She looked around for someone who understood. She did not even feel sufficient pity for his children.

In the evening the funeral car arrived to take her home. She asked to be driven to Academy Street. She was hoping for something, a visitation. She sat in the parked car, behind the tinted windows, his countless footsteps echoing in the streets around her. The echoes of other mothers' sons too, and no bodies for souvenirs. She tapped the driver and he drove on, crossing Sherman, Broadway, towards the park. She remembered summer evenings, old men playing chess under trees, a winter's day when he was four and ran out onto the frozen pond and fell through the ice, a clean vertical drop, almost soundless.

Twilight came. The car turned around, drove south. The city was lighting up. She wondered if he had seen amazing things, nearing death. He, who had been a child of wonder, must have felt astral, aerial, metaphysical. Had the sun spun before him? Had his hands glowed white and luminous? Had he fallen, or fled from flames, his bladder failing, his bowels evacuating, but all of his past—every hour—still contained within him? She began to ponder the precise instant of his death, the tiny subtle intuition when he knew for certain he was going to die. His petrified gaze into midair, beyond the threshold of consciousness into the deepest center of the stars, and then the silent folding, the inward motion, the dissolution into the dark biosphere. How had that moment not registered in her? How had she not felt a disturbance that morning, a little quiver of the self? She closed her eyes. She longed to reach him, lift him under the arms, drape him over her. She looked out the car window, the hum of the engine beneath her. Above her, a sea of tiny stars lighting the sky. She had been here before: nighttime, being ferried through the streets, enclosed and alone like this. And then it came to her. Stendhal. Mathilde, inside her black-draped carriage with the head of her beloved Julien on her lap, while outside the priests escort his bier to the grave. Then, in the depths of the night, burying his head with her own hands.

There was no sign of Monkey. She stood often at her window looking down on the enclosed courtyard with the single tree. Sometimes at dusk she thought she saw him moving in the boughs. She could not sleep. The tolling of bells made her cry. She was always a heartbeat away from brokenness. Does the body go on feeling after death?

She walked a lot, mostly in the evenings. Her feet led her back to Academy Street. She stood on the sidewalk, keeping vigil. She looked up at her old window. There, she had been happy. There, where the air of the outside world did not infiltrate. She lingered, as if waiting for a flare from the window, a sign for where to go next. One afternoon she stood across from the school, under a tree, as parents gathered at the door. In an upstairs classroom, the lights were on, the heads of children visible, and, as she watched, a little hand was raised in answer, lowered again. One day from a bus she saw him. She got off and rushed back, her heart beating wildly. She searched the street, frantic, peered into stores. Back and forth she trudged along the sidewalk, crying. She entered a church where a congregation was gathered for a funeral. She sat in a pew, stood, knelt, prayed for the dead man whose photograph sat on the coffin. At the end, with incense wafting in the air, she stepped into the aisle and walked with the mourners behind the coffin.

The talk was relentless. On the TV, the radio, in the streets—everywhere—the clamor, the arguments, the outrage, the heroes and the villains, all tormenting her. She wanted none of it, wanted the world to go mute. At night it rained. In the mornings the city gleamed. She tried to return to her books, but had little will. She was afraid of certain thoughts, of being devoured by certain thoughts. She began to dread nightfall, heartbreaking twilights. She drew down the blinds, shut out the city. His name resounded in her rooms, in her footsteps, a chant, an echo, a hide-and-seek cry. *The-o, The-o.*

"Do you believe in an afterlife?" she asked Willa. It was December and she had gone to visit Darius. She sat by his bedside. His skin was stretched dry and tight over his bones, his voice little more than a whisper. Afterwards she and Willa walked in the park. It was cold. The cold got into her bones these days. She had been wondering lately about God, if He had been merely a habit in her life. "Or do we only have this life?"

Willa considered the question. "Oh, God, Tess, if there's no afterlife . . . I don't know."

They walked on in silence. She pulled up her collar. When he was small she had told Theo about Claire, his aunt in Heaven. For a while afterwards, he had been obsessed with Heaven. *Will you be you and I be me in Heaven? How will I find you in the crowd? Will we be jealous in Heaven?*

No, Theo, there's no jealousy in Heaven.

"Maybe I'm just a coward," Willa said. "But I'm hedging my bets. Why—what are you thinking, Tess?"

She had always had an inkling, an awareness of something other. God, she supposed. Even as a child, she had been in the habit of awe, drawn to the sacred, to lyrical intuitions and distant heavens. She thought of her mother and father now. She would, if she were to meet her father again, be a little afraid. In his presence she would be a child again.

"I don't know. Life goes by so quickly. Nothing seems to make much sense anymore. But I have to believe, Willa. I have to believe. Because I cannot bear the thought of never seeing Theo again."

She began to cry inside. If he had died young, if he had drowned in the pond that day, how much he would have been spared. He would have been spared his catastrophic ending. As it was now, he had been spared old age. She remembered patients nearing the end in the hospital and the great effort, the immense straining, that each body made to hold on to life. Had his life, his thirty-seven years, counted for something? Had it been enough?

They came upon a dead bird on the path, tiny, stiff, its little chest upturned to the world. They stood before it in silence. She was arrested by grief, and pity. Willa poked it with her shoe, and then withdrew, her thoughts likely with Darius then. She would soon be his widow, his witness on earth. There was no name for what she, Tess, was: an old childless mother. There would be no witness to her life. No Claire, no Theo. Oliver was probably gone too, lying in some potter's field.

She spent Christmas with Jennifer and the children. They would soon forget her, drift from her life. One night in January, she woke in the dark. A shadow crossed the room. Theo, come in search of the missing half of his soul, she thought, yearning to be re-united. She remained very still, waiting. With every breath she edged a little closer to her last. *Please.*

In the morning the light was different. She turned her head. There, outside on the window ledge, sat Monkey. She jumped out of bed and let him in. Warily, he watched her. Then he came and rubbed against her legs, and when she bent to stroke him, her tears flooded back.

Snow fell at Easter. On the streets the wind buffeted from all sides. One morning, the seasons changed. In her kitchen she brewed coffee, split an English muffin, slid it into the toaster. The radio was on.

She poured her coffee, raised her mug. Could a woman sit in her kitchen and drink coffee and wait for a muffin to pop in her toaster, and then smother it with apple jelly and bite into it and not weep for her dead son lost beneath the rubble? Could she listen to the news, the weather, the stock reports, the live phone-ins full of grief and outrage, and mentally calculate what her stock was worth? And still be a mother?

The pale sun streamed in, fell on the pot of jelly, and for a second she felt herself halted. In all her life she had never really known what to do or how to act. She had always been waiting for something or someone to guide her, and age had not altered that essential self.

❖ ❖ ❖

She returned, once, to Easterfield. It was May and she went back for Denis's funeral. His son Michael met her at Shannon and swept her along newly built highways, through towns and vil-lages whose names she could barely recall. He turned onto the avenue at Easterfield and they drove slowly in dappled light under the trees. She would know this place anywhere on earth. She would feel it forever in her bones, every stick and stone of it.

The old house was gone. Denis had built a bungalow thirty years earlier and they were all assembled there. Evelyn, Maeve, widows now, their families. Denis's widow, his grown children, all seated around the coffin. Grandchildren wandering in from the garden. They all embraced her. Her sisters cried, whispered, "Sorry." She touched Denis's cold hands and blessed herself.

She could not, at first, find her bearings. She felt herself among strangers, kind curious strangers. She sat in the unfamiliar kitchen and the talk flowed, words upon words. She wondered if the past was real at all, and what, if anything, remained of it, apart from pain, the memory of pain—its vestiges, like old stumps. She thought how distant the dead had become, lost in the haze of time, the disappeared. Theo had not disappeared. He was close, even as she sat there, as close to her as her jugular vein.

Evelyn looked at her. "You never found Oliver," she said.

She shook her head. She stood accused, and somehow culpable. But Evelyn took her hand. "Claire, Oliver . . . And your own boy, Tess . . . all gone, and so young . . . Do you know what? All America ever brought this family was misfortune."

In the afternoon people came to pay their respects. She walked outside. All of the outbuildings—the coach house, the barns, the arch leading to the orchard—were intact. She felt at a loss for the house but she could not blame Denis—it had been impossible to maintain, and had fallen derelict and dangerous after they had moved out. One does one's best for one's family.

She entered the orchard, entered a great silence, a farm girl again, scarcely disturbed by time. The old fruit trees bent low, ivy-covered, stunted. She walked to the far end and leaned against the wall. The stones were warm, mellow from hundreds of years' sun, acquiescent. She laid her head back and she was caught by something—the flicker of sky, intimations of eternity—and for one pure moment she was free and everything was revealed and everything resolved, the final question—the only question—resolved, and she was being delivered, given her first fleeting glimpse of landfall. A fall of memories loosened and images of happiness returned. Afternoons with Captain and Mike Connolly, her father in a straw hat in a yellow hayfield, her mother at an upstairs window, Oliver at her breast. The lull of Eden, of ancient perfection. Had this been her destination all along, this return to the source, the starting point, the only place she had ever belonged?

She crossed the courtyard and turned the corner, half expecting to come upon new miracles. But there was nothing there, no stamp, no stones. The ground where the house had stood was an L-shaped patch of grass, indistinguishable from the lawn but for its deeper shade of green. Old slates lay stacked against the fowlhouse. To the right, the laurel tree, patient, majestic. In the distance the avenue of beech trees and the lone ash, blue-green and brooding in the evening light, and, further off, the copse by the quarry, the loamy fields. She stood on the edge of the grass. She hovered between worlds, deciphering the ground, tracing in midair the hall, the dining room, the stairs. She was despairingly close to home now, to the rooms and the voices that contained the first names for home. Memories abounded and her heart pounded and history broke in. A famine hospital with a stained-glass window. Bodies in a quarry, smoking in lime. The deeper she went the further she was drawn, into a lower world with the sound of a gong and a mother coughing up blood. A marble fireplace. Adam-and-Eve wallpaper. A red lamp under the back stairs as death rattled upstairs, and the die was cast. The die was cast. A mirror sheathed in black then. And the Garden of Eden plucked and plundered by a blackbird, toppled by a wrecking ball—and Adam, Eve, the apple and the angel, all fallen, vanquished, all buried beneath the rubble.

The cortege followed the hearse up the avenue and turned right onto the main road. For half a mile they drove along Easterfield's perimeter wall. This was it. This was her life, the summation of her life, her dreams run out. She would not encounter love again. She would not lie down with a man or hold a child in her arms. She was at the end of her destiny. She turned her head, looked down over the open sloping fields, with the avenue on the right and groves of old trees, oak and beech, in the distance, and then she leaned forward, her eyes drawn to the slate roofs and stone walls of the outbuildings, the courtyard, the orchard. And then she saw it, the gap where the house had been, the absence at the center of things. An absence that was an injury, a scar on the land. She put her hand to her heart. The house was gone, turned to dust. The earth was mortally wounded. She felt the distress, the long un-rest, the silent suffering of the fields and the beasts, the barns, the grieving ground, and the walls and the trees with the little birds in the boughs all gathered around, bowing down in sorrow.

That night she dreamt. She heard the land weeping. At dawn she heard the clarion call of the city. Streets waiting for her foot-steps. Doors to be opened, books to be read, her life as it had been. And all the days to be got through, the endless days, the nights, the silent rooms. There was no Eden, there would be no

Eden, no radiant streaming, no transformation. Just time, and tasks made lighter by the memory of love, and days like all others when she would put one foot in front of the other and walk on, obedient to fate.

As they drove away, Michael slowed on the avenue, beeped the horn, waved. His children were playing in a corner of the field, on rope swings hung from trees. They were swinging high, back and forth, leaning, reaching out over the quarry, over broken rock and weeds and old water. When they saw their father they swayed in mid-air, raised their little hands, and waved back.

THE AUTHOR IS GRATEFUL
TO THE
ARTS COUNCIL OF IRELAND
FOR ITS
GENEROUS SUPPORT.

A Note About the Author

Mary Costello grew up in the west of Ireland. Her first book, a collection of short stories titled *The China Factory*, was nominated for the Guardian First Book Award. She lives in Dublin.